Candles in my Window

BETH FIRESTONE

Targum Press

First published 1990

ISBN 0-944070-23-X

Phototypeset at Targum Press

Published by:
Targum Press Inc.
22700 W. Eleven Mile Rd.
Southfield, Mich. 48034

Distributed by:
Z. Berman Books
4520 17th Avenue
Brooklyn, N.Y. 11204
(718) 871-5316

Distributed in Israel by:
Nof Books Ltd.
POB 23646
Jerusalem 91235

Printed in Israel

This book is dedicated

- to my husband, Marc, for not letting me give up
- to my parents, for raising me with the values which eventually led me to Torah
- to my daughters, Ariella and Lital, for inspiring me to write this book for their benefit and the benefit of other children
- to Rabbi Zelig Pliskin, for helping to make this book happen
- to Aish HaTorah, for igniting the flames of my own candles in the window.

Chapter 1

IT was a typical weekday night. My mother was in the kitchen getting dinner ready, mumbling to herself about my dad being late...again. Mandy, my little sister, was pulling pots out of the cabinet and banging on them with spoons, singing "Twinkle, Twinkle, Little Star" at the top of her lungs. Sheila, my older sister, was talking on the phone and eating a carrot so loudly you could have heard her chewing in China. I was setting the table, hoping my father would come home soon so my parents wouldn't have an argument.

At seven o'clock, when my dad still wasn't home, my mother told us to sit down for dinner.

"What about Dad?" Sheila asked. I shot her a warning glance. Sometimes she was so caught up in her own little world that she didn't see what was going on around her. She bit her lower lip, realizing she shouldn't have said anything. But it was too late. She'd already pushed my mom's "button."

Mom started up in that uptight voice she used when she was trying to control herself. "If he can't get home in time, he'll just have to eat cold food. Ow! Darn it!" she yelled as she dropped a pot of hot spaghetti sauce on the counter with a big thud.

"There's a hole in the oven mitt," Sheila offered.

"Thanks a lot," Mom muttered as she ran her hand under cold water.

We were having spaghetti, which was usually my favorite supper. But at the moment I didn't feel much like eating. I hate it when my mom's mad at my dad.

By the time my father got home we were already halfway through dinner. I could tell right away that he was happy about something because he kissed each one of us. He hardly ever did that. But Mom was angry and didn't even look at him. She decided to pick on me instead.

"Libby, if you don't stop playing with your food I'm going to send you away from the table without dessert. Finish what's on your plate."

I looked down at my food. I didn't realize I'd been cutting my spaghetti up into a million tiny pieces. By now it looked like a pile of dead worms. I always played with my food when I was nervous. "I don't want dessert," I said.

"You don't have a choice."

"Whoever heard of a mother forcing a kid to eat dessert? I can just see the headlines: 'MOTHER FORCES CHILD TO EAT EVERYTHING ON HER PLATE AND DESSERT. CHILD CHOKES ON CHOCOLATE CHIP AND DIES!' "

This time, Sheila motioned for me to stop. But what was I supposed to do, just sit there? It wasn't fair for Mom to be taking her anger out on me.

My mother was about to respond, but Mandy started bouncing up and down in her high chair screaming, "Pischetti! Pischetti!" so Mom got up to get her some more.

Dad sat down and started to help himself to dinner. He was acting like nothing was wrong. Mom still hadn't said anything.

"How is everybody?" my father asked.

"Okay, if you like eating worms," I muttered.

Sheila gave me a "you better keep quiet" look and slurped a long strand of spaghetti into her mouth.

"Sheila, don't slurp," my father said.

"You never learn, do you?" Mom finally confronted him.

Dad looked up from his plate. "Oh come on, Doris. Not tonight. Besides, when you hear what happened—"

"Not tonight?" she interrupted. "So when? Tomorrow? The night after? Is it ever going to change?" Her voice was getting louder and louder.

I looked at Sheila. She was biting her nails, a nervous habit of hers that drove me crazy. Neither of us wanted to hear them fight. I never knew whose side to be on. My mother was so upset she didn't notice that she was spooning food into Mandy's mouth too fast for her to swallow. Mandy started to squirm.

"Tonight is different. I have something to tell

everyone," my father said, trying to stay calm. But just at that moment Mandy started to cry.

"Look what you're doing to her!" my father snapped, losing control. Mom looked at Mandy. There was mashed spaghetti all over her bib and more dripping out of her mouth. You could really lose your appetite around my house.

"If you can do it better, then why don't you? I'm sick and tired of being the bad guy all the time," my mother said, wiping Mandy's face so hard that she started to cry even louder. It was getting pretty unbearable.

"You feed the baby for a change," Mom declared, standing up. "And you clear the table and wash the dishes and help the kids get ready for bed. I'm going to the study, which is what I've been meaning to do all day! And Libby, you're going to sit there until you've finished every last bite!" She stormed out of the kitchen and off to the study. That's where her computer was. Before Mom had gotten pregnant with Mandy, she'd been taking writing classes at the university. Since Mandy had come along, she hadn't had much time to write and was always complaining about it.

Sheila got up, lifted Mandy out of her high chair, and took her into the other room. I was alone with my father. He just stared down at his plate of cold spaghetti, twirling it with his fork, not eating. Finally he looked up at me.

"I was going to tell everyone that I got a promotion."

"That's great Dad," I said, feeling pretty bad

that I was the only one around to hear the good news.

"It means we'll be moving to Los Angeles," he continued.

Moving? The word echoed over and over in my ears. Los Angeles? That was clear across the country. My heart started beating really fast and my hands got all clammy.

"I'm going to be a vice president. It's a big promotion."

Who cared about a stupid promotion if it meant we had to move? "But I like it here. I don't want to move," I started to protest.

"You just think you don't, Libby. Wait until you see how much better our lives will be. We'll be able to send you to the best private schools, and give you piano lessons. And you'll have your very own room."

Where did parents come up with these ideas? I'd never asked for piano lessons. And I liked my school here. This was where all my friends were. My father promised I'd make new friends in Los Angeles. But what did he know about being eleven years old?

He went on and on about how great the place was, but I wasn't convinced. I loved it in Connecticut. I loved living across the street from a farm. I loved the snowy winters and the leaves changing colors in the fall. Los Angeles was like one big summer all year long. And it was smoggy and crowded and you couldn't trust anybody. Jenny Tucker, a girl in my class, had moved to Connecticut from Los

Angeles and she'd told me that. She couldn't believe it when she first came here and found out nobody ever locked his door. She said she wouldn't trade living here for all the money in the world.

"I give up," my father finally muttered. "What do you think I've been working so hard for?" he said as he left the kitchen. I felt kind of sorry for him. He did work really hard. The problem was, he worked so hard that we hardly ever saw him.

I looked down at my plate of spaghetti, if that's what you could still call it. It made me sick just to look at it. I started to clear the table. I could hear my mother typing away in the study. I wondered what she was writing and why she wanted to be in there so much more than she wanted to be out here. I could hear my father blasting his opera in the den like he always did when he was upset. Sheila and Mandy were watching T.V. upstairs. How come I was stuck doing the dishes? If everyone else could be upset, why couldn't I? I left the rest of the dishes and went upstairs to tell Sheila the news.

"We'll see about that!" she cried. "I'm going to be a junior next year. I'm a cheerleader. They can't pull me away from here just like that!" She stomped out of the room and downstairs to my parents.

I picked Mandy up and carried her downstairs. I felt like going outside. It was the beginning of summer so the days were getting longer and it was still light out. When I reached the bottom of the stairs I could hear the loud voices of Sheila and my parents in the study. I took Mandy outside with me and we sat on the lawn, where we could look at the farm across the road and the river beyond. You could bet our backyard in Los Angeles wouldn't look half as beautiful as this. After a while Sheila came outside and sat there with us. She looked sad and defeated and her eyes were all red from crying.

"Mom thinks it's the greatest news in the world," she reported.

"She does?"

"She says Hollywood is the best place for a writer."

"Is that all she ever thinks about?"

"And she won't have to shovel snow in the winter."

"But what about us? What about what *we* want?" I said.

"What about it?" Sheila said bitterly as she chewed on her pinky nail. I could tell she was trying to hold back tears. I could feel a big lump rising in my own throat so I didn't say anything more.

We just sat quietly, staring out at the farm and the river, watching the sky grow dark and waiting for the first star to come out so we could make a wish on it. I doubted it would do any good.

Chapter 2

MY father meant it when he said we'd be moving into a big house. It was one of those very modern kinds you see in magazines, with high ceilings and lots of huge windows all over the place. It was hard to get used to, especially having my own room. I guess I liked the privacy, but I didn't always like sleeping alone at night. Sometimes I snuck into Mandy's room and brought her in to sleep with me.

My father meant it about the piano lessons, too. Actually, I liked playing the piano. My teacher said I had natural talent and perfect pitch. That meant I could hum any note she told me to without hearing it played first.

Our house was on a street with a lot of other big houses. In Connecticut there were always kids playing outside and we knew who lived in every house on our street. Here you hardly ever saw anyone outside and everybody drove when he wanted to go somewhere. In fact, the driveways and front lawns were so big and far away from each other, you'd have to use a megaphone just to say hello to the person living across the street.

Everything had changed but one thing—our family. Dad was even busier than before with his new job and hardly ever got home in time to have dinner with us. Mom just finally resigned herself to it and didn't even bother waiting anymore. At least we didn't have to listen to them fight about it.

Not that they didn't manage to find other things to fight about. One night, not long after we'd moved in, they got into a big argument. They were in the study and the door was closed, but Sheila and I could hear them. The neighbors probably could, too, for that matter. I'd never heard my mother sound quite so upset. She was saying she couldn't do it all...cook, clean, decorate the house, take care of us, and write. After a while their voices grew quiet and all you could hear was mumbling. At least they were working it out. Boy, were they. Little did I know that the next day we'd be getting a live-in housekeeper. Mom said it was the answer to all our problems. Maybe her problems.

Our new housekeeper's name was Quana and she was from Mexico. She spoke a little English but not much. It was weird having someone we didn't even know always around, and I tried to avoid her. But Mandy took an instant liking to her and followed her everywhere.

A few days after Quana came Mom decided to stick me in summer school. This was all on account

of Sheila. She'd gotten a D in math and needed to
make it up, so I had to suffer, too. At least she let
me choose what classes I wanted to take. I decided
on music and math. Unlike Sheila, I think math is
fun. I was the only girl in my math class and all the
girls in my music class already knew each other.
They were cliquey and didn't make it very easy for
me to break in. It's not that I was a nerd or something. Or that I didn't have anything interesting to
say. I'd just never been very good at making friends.

*   *   *

Just as I was beginning to think that Mom had
locked herself away in her study for good, I got
home from school one day to find her packing up
the car with a picnic basket, a beach umbrella, towels,
and rafts.

"Go get your bathing suit on," she said. "We're
going to the beach." That was the one exciting
thing about California. I'd never seen the ocean,
and I'd been bugging my mom every day to take
us. Finally, we were going! Sheila and I got ready
in no time at all and jumped into the car. Quana
came out carrying Mandy and put her in her car
seat. Then, to my surprise, she got into the car
with us.

I didn't say anything, but I was disappointed. I
had hoped it would be a family outing—just the
four of us, like old times. Oh well, at least Mom
was taking time off to be with us.

But no sooner had we arrived at the beach and

unloaded everything than Mom said she'd be back to pick us up in two hours. She said something in Spanish to Quana, kissed Mandy goodbye, and was off.

Sheila didn't seem to mind. Or if she did, she didn't want to show it. She's pretty good at that. But I minded. I was really beginning to wonder why my parents had kids at all. I mean, what was the point if they were never going to spend any time with us? I walked slowly down to the ocean, not feeling very excited about it anymore. I stuck my feet into the water. It was cold and Sheila was wading up to her knees, trying to get used to it. Suddenly I felt so angry, I just dove right in. I wasn't even afraid of the waves. I let one knock me over and jostle me around. It felt like the ocean was as angry as I was.

When I got out of the water, Sheila was already with some kids she knew from summer school. I was kind of jealous that she'd made friends so easily. I could see she was going to blend in well here with her tan skin and long, blond hair. Unfortunately, my curly, dark hair and freckles weren't exactly the coolest look in California. I really missed Connecticut. People there didn't care so much about appearances. Not that I thought I was ugly or anything. But it didn't seem fair that Sheila should be instantly popular just because she had inherited my mother's genes. Why don't people care more about what's inside a person—what he thinks and feels about things? That's what makes a person who he is. Not what he looks like. That's what I always care about, anyway.

I knew Sheila wouldn't want me tagging along so I built a sand castle with Quana and Mandy. I hoped I'd make a friend soon before I went crazy. I really needed someone to talk to.

Chapter 3

I don't know what got into me that day. And little did I know it would be a day I'd never forget.

I was practicing the piano. I'd already learned six scales and I could play one of Bach's easy sonatas for advanced beginners. I loved to play. I'd just started on my E scales when Abby, my mom's new writing partner, came into the room.

"Honey," she said (she calls everybody "honey"), "could you do that later? We're on a very important call and I can't hear anything with all that banging in the background."

Banging? This was music, you uncultured creep! I practically had to bite my tongue to keep myself from saying something I shouldn't. "Don't call me 'honey,' " I mumbled as I walked past her.

"What did you say?"

I didn't answer. I didn't owe her any explanations. She wasn't my mother.

It was funny how things changed. When I first

met Abby I thought she was the prettiest person I'd ever seen. Her skin was always perfectly tanned and her nails were real long and painted pink. She had the biggest diamond ring I'd ever seen and she always wore clothes that looked very expensive. I can remember the first time I met her. I answered the door and there she was, looking like something straight out of one of Sheila's fashion magazines.

"Oh my God, you're as beautiful as your mother!" she said. "Hi, sweetheart, I'm Abby." She kissed me and walked into the house. "I'm going to steal you away from your mother and take you all around Los Angeles and tell everyone you're mine. How about it? Now, where are you hiding your other sisters?" She met Sheila and Mandy and called them "sweetie" and "honey" and told my mother she was going to take us all on an outing soon.

Not long after that first meeting I overheard Abby say that she didn't know how my mom dealt with three kids, and that deciding not to have children was the best decision she'd ever made. Abby was divorced.

"At least I got something from that man," she said when my mother admired her big diamond ring. Abby didn't seem so pretty to me anymore and we still hadn't been on any outing.

After her last comment on my piano playing, I decided to ask my mother if I could go to the ice cream store a few blocks away. After all, they didn't want me around here. But when she saw me she put her finger to her lips and waved me away.

"But I just wanted—" I started to say.

"Shh. Not now," she whispered and turned her back to me.

"It's always not now," I said. But she just shook her head so hard it looked like it might fall off. I opted for our freezer instead but there was nothing there. Not even a Popsicle. Nothing was going my way that afternoon. No ice cream, no money, no piano, no mother, nobody to play with. If I'd jumped off the roof and died I bet nobody would have even noticed.

I poured myself a glass of milk and sat down at the kitchen table. That's when I spotted Abby's purse sitting wide open on a kitchen chair. I'd never stolen anything before, not even from my own parents. But as I caught sight of Abby through the crack in the door, gabbing away on the phone, I became angry. Not only did I never see my mother because she was always locked away in the study with her, but now Abby was acting like she owned our house! Before I knew what I was doing I reached into her purse and grabbed her wallet. She had a lot of cash. I took a ten-dollar bill and ran out of the house. I told myself she was rich and would never miss it. Besides, she deserved it.

I headed for the shopping center a few blocks away. As if everything that had happened so far wasn't enough, on my way I saw Sheila and some of her new friends sitting on the hood of a car. It was parked in the driveway of a big, two-story brick house. Then a girl came running out of the house waving car keys and crying, "I found them!"

Everybody cheered and jumped into the car, and they drove off really fast. I quickly turned down another street so they wouldn't see me. Sheila wasn't yet sixteen and only had her learner's permit. She could only drive with a parent along. The girl in the driver's seat didn't look old enough to be driving alone either. The whole thing smelled funny to me. I felt like I should tell my parents but I knew Sheila'd never forgive me if I did. Besides, who was I to tattle on her when I'd just stolen ten dollars?

Chapter 4

AS I approached the ice cream store, I could see an old woman standing outside with her hand outstretched. She was what the news called a "bag lady." She looked very poor and dirty and stood by a big shopping cart filled with junk. I always wonder how people get that way. I always imagine that they were once cute little babies like Mandy. She was asking people for money, but nobody was stopping to give her any. Her fingers were really crooked and her hand had scabs on it. I was afraid she might touch me, so as I walked past her, I did what everyone else did: I sped up and looked away, then went into the ice cream store as fast as I could. I bought a double cone and sat down to eat it. But I couldn't help looking back out the window at her.

I felt kind of bad sitting there eating my ice cream while she was out there begging. She was probably hungry. Watching her took my appetite away and I was about to throw the rest of my cone away and leave when a girl who looked about my age approached the store. She was with a small boy, her brother maybe. He wore a little black beanie on his head. I knew it meant he was Jewish and I knew there was a name for those beanies, but I couldn't remember it. I was Jewish but we didn't go to temple or anything.

The bag lady asked them for money and I watched curiously as the girl actually stopped and reached into her pocket. She took out some money and handed it to the bag lady with a smile.

"God bless you," the lady said.

"Thank you. God bless you, too," the girl answered. She was thanking the lady!

She'd made it seem so easy. Why couldn't I have done that? I watched them enter the store and order a quart of ice cream to take home and a single cone for each of them to eat now. But when it was time to pay they didn't seem to have enough money.

"But a quart is $3.50," the girl said.

"Look again," the man behind the counter replied. "Prices went up two days ago." The girl looked at the list of prices on the wall, then told the man she would have to run home to get some more money. I couldn't believe it. Because they'd given money to the bag lady they didn't have enough to pay for the ice cream!

Before I knew what I was doing I darted up to the counter.

"Here," I said, shoving a five-dollar bill into the man's hand. "This will cover it."

"You can't do that," the girl protested.

"Why not?"

"I don't even know you. And besides, we have more money at home."

"You can pay me back then," I said. It was as if someone else were talking, not me. I didn't know what had gotten into me. It had been a really strange day: first I steal money from my mother's friend, then I spend it buying ice cream for a girl I don't even know.

The girl looked at me shyly. "Okay. But only if you walk home with me right now and let me pay you back," she said.

"Okay," I agreed.

Once outside, the girl told me she lived on Maple Street. It was in the opposite direction of my house.

"Thank you for doing that," she said as we began walking.

"You're welcome," I said, smiling at her. She smiled back. We walked a little farther in silence. The houses were getting smaller and there were apartment buildings around.

"What's your name?" I finally asked.

"Rebecca."

"I'm Aaron," her brother said loudly, running ahead of us.

"What's yours?" Rebecca asked.

"Libby."

We smiled at each other and walked a bit more.

"We're just a few more blocks," Rebecca said quietly.

I started noticing kids playing outside in front

of their houses. This was the first time I'd seen that in Los Angeles. The boys all wore those beanies.

"Why do they wear those caps?" I asked.

Rebecca didn't look at me. She didn't answer right away either. In fact, she was acting kind of funny. Almost like she was afraid to talk to me or something.

"You're not Jewish, right?" she finally asked.

Now what had made her think that? I told her that I was, in fact, Jewish.

"Oh...I'm sorry," she said, blushing.

"No big deal," I said. "I was just wondering why they wore those funny-looking beanies."

Rebecca giggled to herself. "They're called *kippot*," she said, still not looking at me when she talked. I'm shy, too, but at least I look at people when I talk to them. Why was she acting so peculiar?

"Aaron, slow down!" she called.

We walked a ways without saying anything and then I told her I thought it was nice that she'd given money to the bag lady.

"You're always supposed to give *tzedakah* when somebody asks," she responded.

"What?" I had no idea what she was talking about.

"I thought you said you were Jewish," she said, finally looking up from the ground at me.

"I am. So what?" I still didn't know why she was making such a big fuss about being Jewish.

"And you don't know about the *mitzvah* of *tzedakah*?"

"The what of what?" I asked.

"*Tzedakah*. You know...charity?"

"Oh. Why didn't you just say so in the first place?"

"It's a *mitzvah*," she continued.

I shook my head, not knowing what she meant. What language was she speaking, anyway?

"You don't know what a *mitzvah* is?" Rebecca said, looking at me like I was the crazy one!

"Look, maybe I should just go home," I said. I didn't need some know-it-all looking down her nose at me. I stopped walking and started to turn back in the direction we'd come from.

"No...wait...I'm sorry," Rebecca stammered. I turned and looked at her. She bit her lower lip and scratched the back of her leg with her foot. "It was nice of you to pay for my ice cream. I want to pay you back."

I did want the money back. And even though I was beginning to think she was kind of strange, I was also a little curious. There was something so different about her. "Oh, all right," I said, and we started to walk together again.

"I don't have any friends who aren't *frum*," Rebecca said.

Oh no, here we go again. "*Frum?*" I asked, having never heard that word.

"Oh...sorry," Rebecca apologized. "I mean Orthodox...you know, religious," she explained.

"Oh...is that what you are?"

"Yes."

I figured that had something to do with why she seemed so uncomfortable around me. I was as different from her as she was from me. "Well you're right about that. I'm not...*frum*," I said, trying out the new word. "I've never even been to temple."

"Never?"

"Nope...what's the big deal, anyway?"

Her face turned all red. "No big deal," she said. I couldn't quite figure her out.

We walked another block without saying anything. After all, I'd never met an Orthodox Jew before and I really didn't know what to say.

"What's a *mitzvah*?" I finally asked, thinking about what she'd said.

"There are 613 *mitzvot*!" Aaron shouted out.

"Shh, Aaron," Rebecca said, pushing her brother on ahead of us. "*Mitzvot* are things God commands us Jews to do," she answered.

So how come I'd never heard of them? "You have a direct line with God or something?" I asked jokingly.

Rebecca laughed. "Not quite. The *mitzvot* are written in the Torah," she explained.

I didn't know what the Torah was and looked at her questioningly.

"You know, the Bible," she said when she saw that I didn't understand.

"Oh. Why didn't you just say so?" I said. "Anyway, I've never read it, so I wouldn't know about the *mitzvot*."

"Well it's all there in the Bible...and this is where we live," Rebecca said, stopping in front of a two-story duplex. "We're upstairs."

When we got to the top of the stairs Aaron

burst into the house screaming, "Ema! Rebecca brought a girl home. We gave *tzedakah* and couldn't pay for the ice cream! She didn't even know what a *mitzvah* is!"

There were a lot of toys scattered on the floor, and a little girl about Mandy's age was sitting in the middle of the living room playing. It was much smaller than our house. One long wall was nothing but bookcases filled with hundreds of books. There was a couch and two chairs that looked kind of old and worn, not at all like our new living room furniture, which my mom never let us sit on. There were pictures of different men with long beards on another wall. We moved into the dining room, where there was a very long, wooden table and chairs, and another bookcase with more books. There were a lot of windows everywhere and sunlight poured into the house. I liked it here. It had a cheerful feeling. I heard banging in the kitchen and it smelt like someone had been baking.

"What girl?" Rebecca's mother, or "Ema" as they called her, walked out of the kitchen. She wore a colorful scarf on her head and I could see she was pregnant. "Who's this?" she asked, smiling at me.

"Libby," Rebecca answered. "She paid for the ice cream."

"Hi, Libby. I'm Mrs. Klein. Now Rebecca, please start from the beginning."

As Rebecca related what happened, we followed Mrs. Klein into the kitchen and she gave us some cake and milk. Aaron and Chana, the baby, joined us, and soon there was a lot of talking and commotion in the kitchen as Mrs. Klein cooked and Rebecca's brother and sister played. Rebecca wasn't acting so shy anymore and after a little while we were talking about all different things. I found out she'd spent a few years in upstate New York, so she knew exactly how I felt when I told her I missed Connecticut. We both loved the snow. I started to feel a lot better. In fact, I was feeling so good that I forgot I'd stolen the ten dollars from Abby. I didn't remember until Rebecca's mother gave me back the money for the ice cream. That's when I realized I'd been away for a few hours and my mother was sure to miss me. I stood up to leave.

"Ema, can she come for Shabbat?" Rebecca asked her mother.

"I don't see why not," Mrs. Klein replied.

"Will you ask your mother if you can come?" Rebecca said to me.

"Shabbat?" I said, almost afraid to ask.

Rebecca looked at her mother, and for a moment nobody said anything. Boy, did I feel dumb. Then again, it wasn't my fault I didn't know about any of this Jewish stuff.

"The best way to learn about Shabbat is to experience it," Mrs. Klein finally said, breaking the silence.

"Yeah," Rebecca agreed. "Just come over Friday afternoon and you'll see. It's really fun. And plan on sleeping over."

Wow! Not only had I made a new friend, but she was already inviting me for a sleepover! I promised to ask my mother and call Rebecca to let her know. When I left their house I started to run. But then I started to think about what I'd done and I slowed down to a walk. What if Abby was still there and she had noticed the money was gone? And my mother was sure to be mad that I had left without her permission. I was in for a double whammy. So, what did it matter if I was a few more minutes late?

Chapter 5

AS I opened the front door I could hear noises coming from the kitchen. I tiptoed as fast as I could into my room. Just as I was opening the door to my room, Mandy came around the corner.

"Libby!" she cried. "Hi, Libby!" She ran over and hugged my legs.

"Shh!" I said, lifting her up and carrying her into my room. A second later Sheila came in.

"Mom said to tell you dinner's ready. What have you been doing in here all day, anyway? You know you really should get out of the house. You're never gonna make friends sitting around in your room all day long doing God knows what."

So they hadn't even missed me. I should have known.

"As a matter of fact, I did make a new friend today. And she has a little sister just about your age," I said to Mandy, giving her a big kiss on her cheek. She threw her arms around my neck and hugged me. Sometimes I loved her so much.

"What'd you do? Stick your head out of the window and holler for a friend?" Sheila taunted.

"I met her at the ice cream store, for your information," I said without thinking.

"The ice cream store? Nobody even knew you were gone. Who said you could go?" Sheila asked with her hands on her hips.

"I guess the same person who told you you could go driving around without a driver's license!" I said before I could stop myself.

"You were spying!"

"I was not! I was just walking that way. I have better things to do than spy on you and your stupid friends."

"They're not stupid. And if you say one word about this to Mom or Dad, I'll tell all my friends you're a fink," she threatened, crinkling her eyes into little slits.

"I wasn't gonna say anything," I said, feeling a weird sensation deep in my stomach. So it was true after all. If my parents knew, they could stop her. But I couldn't be a fink.

"Smart girl," Sheila said, turning to leave.

"If you think it's cool, you're stupid. You could get hurt," I called after her.

"What do you know about being cool?" Sheila said, leaving my room in a huff. We never used to fight like this. She had changed since moving to Los Angeles. I wasn't sure how, but I knew her new friends were only going to make things worse.

*   *   *

"You've been so quiet today, Libby. What have you been up to?" my mother said during dinner. We'd been eating mostly take-out lately and that night was leftovers from last night's Chinese food.

"I made a new friend."

"Terrific. At school?" My mother seemed genuinely happy that I'd finally met someone.

I looked at Sheila, who was shovelling a big piece of soggy egg roll into her mouth. She wouldn't dare say anything. "No. At the park," I said. The park was close enough that I didn't need permission to go. "She invited me for a sleepover this Friday. Can I go?"

"I think that could be arranged. Where does she live?"

"Not too far from here."

My mom was leaning over the table, putting food on her plate to take into the study with her. "Sheila, please feed Mandy," she said. Sheila plopped a bunch of noodles on Mandy's tray. "What's her name?" my mother asked.

"Rebecca. And she's really nice. They have four kids and her mother's pregnant again. They're Jewish and they have Shabbat on Friday nights. Rebecca said it's lots of fun." I was so excited I just kept talking. That is, until I noticed a funny look on my mom's face.

"Where did you say she lives?" my mother asked.

"Near the ice cream store," Sheila said, tempting fate. She gave me a big fake smile and I gave her a dirty look to match.

"Oh, that area," my mother said strangely.

"What's Shabbat, anyway?" I asked.

But my mother didn't answer because she'd suddenly noticed Mandy, who by now had thrown half the noodles on the floor. "Sheila, I told you to feed her!" she snapped.

"I did!" Sheila said.

"Where's Quana? Quana!" my mother yelled.

"It's Quana's day off," I reminded her. "So what's Shabbat?" I asked again. When my mother realized Quana wasn't going to see us through dinner she eventually sat down at the table next to Mandy and started to feed her.

"It's just an old Jewish custom," she finally answered, "and maybe it isn't such a good idea for you to sleep over there. You hardly know these people."

"But you just said I could go! That isn't fair!" I protested, confused by her sudden change of mind.

Lucky for me the phone started to ring and she jumped up to get it. I knew I had her then. "You said I could go, Mom...pleeeaaase?" I begged. My mother looked at me and took a deep breath. The phone rang again. She shook her head. I knew that shake. It meant she didn't have the energy to argue about it anymore. It meant she was going to give in.

"Oh, all right. Just don't mention any of this Shabbat business to your father," she finally said as she picked up the phone.

"I don't get it," I commented to Sheila, momentarily forgetting we were on the outs.

Sheila bit her lip and shook her head as if she was as baffled as I was. "Remember when I slept over at Wendy Schwartz's house and she took me to Hebrew school with her?" she asked.

"Yeah, I remember. You got into a big fight with Dad because he said Wendy's mom should have asked him first before she took you. Then he called Mrs. Schwartz and got mad at her."

"I was so embarrassed," Sheila recalled.

"Why do you think he did that?"

"He would never talk about it with me," she said, getting up to clear her plate. "It's like he's hiding something from us," she added as she left the kitchen.

"Yeah...and I'd sure like to know what," I said out loud to nobody.

That night I lay in bed a long time, thinking of all that had gone on that day. So much had happened! I was feeling pretty guilty about taking the money so I decided to replace it as soon as I could. And I was going to spend Shabbat with my new friend...I guessed she was my friend, even if we were really different. I thought more about my father and wondered why he never talked about being Jewish and why he had never taught us about Shabbat or *tzedakah* or the Torah. I finally fell asleep thinking about Rebecca and her nice family and the wonderful smell of their apartment. I could hardly wait until Friday night.

Chapter 6

I arrived at Rebecca's at around six o'clock. Her sister Sarah answered the door. She looked like she was about eight years old.

"Rebecca's taking a shower," she said to me, then yelled, "EEEMMMAA, that girl's here!"

Mrs. Klein came to the door with Chana in her arms. She seemed out of breath. "Well, let her in, Sarah," she ordered as she put Chana down in the middle of the living room with some toys. "Hello, Libby. Come in. Sarah, why don't you show Libby to your room? And help Aaron get dressed."

The whole apartment smelled like whatever was for dinner. It smelled like it was going to be delicious. Mrs. Klein seemed to be in a big hurry and rushed back to the kitchen. I followed Sarah past the dining room. The table was decorated with a pretty white tablecloth and a vase of flowers.

"And tell Rebecca to hurry up. The table still needs to be set!" Mrs. Klein yelled from the kitchen.

I was a little surprised to see her acting this way. She was hardly the calm, peaceful lady I remembered.

"Don't mind her," Rebecca said, emerging from the bathroom with her head wrapped in a towel. "She always gets crazy before Shabbat. There's so much to do before the sun goes down. Come on in. This is where we sleep."

"Before the sun goes down?" I asked, following her down the hall.

"Shabbat begins at sunset. After that you can't cook or use electricity and...." She stopped herself for a minute, remembering how strange this all must have sounded to me. "Well you just can't do any kind of work," she continued, "and that includes a lot of different things. But you'll see for yourself."

I guessed I would. Everything seemed so foreign and different, almost like I was in another country. I felt a little uncomfortable. At the same time there was something very exciting about it all.

I followed Rebecca into a room with two sets of bunk beds.

"That one is Aaron's, that one is Sarah's, and this one is mine. There's one left over for guests," Rebecca said, pointing to the extra bed.

It was hard to believe they all slept in the same room. Then I remembered that not too long ago I had shared a room with Sheila. Actually, I had liked sharing a room. I never used to get scared at night and it was nice always having someone to talk to...back when Sheila and I were friends. Maybe having our own rooms had something to do with us never talking anymore.

"Rebecca! Sarah! What are you doing in there?" Mrs. Klein screamed from the kitchen.

"I'm getting dressed!" Rebecca called. She looked at me and rolled her eyes. I rolled mine back to show her I understood. No matter how different they were, all mothers were the same when it came to certain things.

I put my bag down and sat on a bed while Rebecca disappeared into her closet. She came back out wearing a pretty white blouse and a light blue skirt. I looked down at my jeans and sweatshirt. I hadn't known I was supposed to get dressed up. Rebecca offered to let me borrow something of hers. She gave me a navy blue skirt and a white, ruffled blouse, just like the one she was wearing. They fit perfectly. We looked at ourselves in the mirror. It was fun being twins. Mrs. Klein called us again and we rushed out.

Sarah had already set out the plates. They looked like the fancy china my mother only used on very special occasions.

"Here." Rebecca handed me some forks that looked like the beautiful silver my mother kept stored away for holidays. Then we took pretty pink napkins and put them in flowered napkin holders. When we finished setting the table we stood back and admired it.

"It looks fit for a queen," I said.

"Well it should," Mrs. Klein remarked, placing

a crystal wine decanter on the table. "The Shabbos Queen."

*   *   *

For the next half hour or so we all helped Mrs. Klein in the kitchen. She put everyone to work, except Chana, who just waddled around under everyone's feet, talking baby talk. Rebecca and I laid out olives and pickles and this weird-smelling stuff called gefilte fish on a big silver platter.

"Don't worry, you don't have to eat it. I never do," Rebecca said.

Everyone was rushing around busily. I never knew helping out like that could be so much fun. "Okay, kids, that about does it," Mrs. Klein finally declared. "I'm hopping in the shower. Everybody better be ready to light when I get out," she said, leaving the kitchen in a whoosh.

"Light?" I asked.

"You'll see in a little while," Rebecca said.

*   *   *

Mrs. Klein came back out about twenty minutes later, wearing a pink and yellow dress with white flowers. She had put on makeup and it really made her look pretty. She wasn't wearing a scarf and her hair looked beautiful. I couldn't imagine how she had washed and set it so fast.

"It takes my mother an hour to look like that," I said.

"It's a *sheitel*," Rebecca whispered.

"A what?" I whispered back, not knowing what she meant.

"She's wearing a wig," Rebecca explained. "She always keeps her hair covered."

But before I could find out more about this, everyone moved into the living room. On a ledge above the fireplace, three sets of candlesticks were neatly lined up.

"This one's for you," Rebecca said, pulling me in front of a brass candlestick with a small, white candle in it. "Just watch us and then I'll help you."

I watched as Mrs. Klein lit two candles for herself and one for Chana, who was too young to light. Sarah and Rebecca lit their own. They all put their hands above the flames and made three graceful circular motions, then covered their eyes. All together they said something in a language I didn't understand. (Later I learned they were speaking Hebrew.) Afterwards Chana started jumping up and down saying, "Good Shabbos! Good Shabbos!"

"Shh, Chana, not yet," Mrs. Klein said. "Libby still has to light."

I felt a little self-conscious as Rebecca showed me what to do. I lit the candles and made three circular motions. Then I repeated the Hebrew words, one at a time, after Rebecca while I covered my eyes. When I finished, the whole family wished each other "good Shabbos."

Mrs. Klein disappeared into the kitchen again and a few minutes later the front door opened. Chana toddled over to her father, shouting "Abba!

Abba!" A man with a bushy beard and mustache reached down to pick her up. Dressed in a black jacket, black pants, a white shirt, and a black hat, he looked a little scary to me if you want to know the truth. But then he smiled at me, and it lit up his whole face.

"You must be Libby," Mr. Klein said. "Welcome."

"Abba! Abba!" Aaron cried as he tugged on his father's pants. Mr. Klein lifted Aaron up and held him upside down while he laughed and yelled for his father to put him down.

"Where's Ema? It's time for *Kiddush*...Ema!" Mr. Klein called, carrying Aaron into the dining room as he kicked and screamed and laughed.

Kiddush? Every time I finished asking one question, somebody did or said something that raised a new one. The more I learned, the harder it was to believe that I'd been Jewish all these years without knowing anything about it.

As everyone followed Mr. Klein into the dining room, I turned to look at all the candles lined up on the ledge one more time. By now the room was dark except for their glow. They looked so beautiful burning there in a neat little row. As I stood watching them, a warm, tingly sensation moved up and down my body. It felt so peaceful in this room. I wouldn't have minded just sitting there in front of the candles for a while but Rebecca called for me to come into the dining room for...*Kiddush?*

Chapter 7

I found out that *Kiddush* is the special blessing said over wine on Shabbat and Jewish holidays. Mr. and Mrs. Klein drank wine and gave us grape juice. Then we washed our hands in the kitchen with a special silver washing cup and said another blessing. Rebecca explained that this was done before eating bread. Back at the table Mr. Klein said a blessing over the special Shabbat bread, called *challah*, and we were finally permitted to eat. A person could starve to death before finishing all the blessings! But it was worth the wait. There were so many delicious foods to eat.

The next day, I found out it was still Shabbat! In fact, it didn't end until the sun went down Saturday night. I also learned that on Shabbat the Kleins didn't turn on and off any lights or listen to music, or do anything that involved electricity. And they didn't answer the phone or drive in their car. I forgot and accidentally turned on the lamp in our bedroom. I wasn't allowed to turn it off again so Mrs. Klein had to cover it so that we would be able to sleep! It all seemed very weird to me, but Rebecca said it was one of God's commandments to keep Shabbat separate from the other days in the week. All of these things reminded us that Shabbat was different. I'll say!

On Saturday morning we went to "shul" — that's what they called the synagogue. The whole place was buzzing with children running around and people talking and praying and the rabbi leading everyone in Hebrew. I was surprised to see that there was a women's side and a men's side. We sat with Rebecca's mother on the women's side, of course.

There was a kind of wall separating the two sides, but it was made of this stuff you could see through a little. I was curious to see what was going on on the men's side so I peeked through. They were all wearing these big, white shawls over their shoulders. (I later learned that this shawl is called a *tallit*.) The men all swayed back and forth, filling the shul with Hebrew songs. I just followed Rebecca as best as I could, standing and sitting when she did and trying to read some of the prayers in English.

Just as I thought my legs would fall off before all this standing and sitting would end, Rebecca took me by the hand and led me down a hall to where a bunch of girls our age were babysitting the smaller children. She introduced me to a few girls and asked them if they were going to the

"*Mitzvah* Project" that afternoon. Oh no, more *mitz-vot....*

As we were walking home Rebecca told me all about the "*Mitzvah* Project." Every summer their class got involved in some kind of *mitzvah*. This summer it was visiting old people who lived in a retirement home. That's where we were going after lunch.

I wasn't sure I liked this idea at all. I didn't like being around old people very much. I had been in one of those homes once to visit my mother's aunt. It smelled funny and all the old ladies wanted to kiss me. They wore tons of awful-smelling perfume and always talked about their aches and pains and asked me the same question at least ten times. I thought of riding my bike home after lunch. After all, I wasn't Orthodox. I could end Shabbat whenever I felt like it. But Rebecca was so excited to have me come along and get involved that before I knew it, after lunch, I was headed out the door with her. It would only be for an hour anyway, so what could it hurt just this once?

As we approached the retirement home I began to wish I'd gone home after all. The sign out front said "Golden Years Retirement Home." They hardly seemed like golden years to me. As we opened the front doors I was hit by the same smell I remembered from my mother's aunt's home. What is that smell?

Inside there were some old people sitting on couches and chairs, not doing much of anything. A few ladies were playing cards and some men were playing checkers. Others were in the dining room. Rebecca's friends all seemed to know what to do, and before long the little room filled with chatter and laughter. I went with Rebecca to the dining room, where her special friend, Mrs. Stein, was sitting at a table by herself. Rebecca greeted her by kissing her cheek. Mrs. Stein's whole face lit up. Rebecca introduced me to her and we both sat down. Then one of the employees came over and asked Mrs. Stein if she was finished yet. He sounded annoyed.

"The meat was all dried out again," Mrs. Stein said. "It was hard to chew."

"All anyone ever does around here is complain," he grumbled and took her plate away.

"They don't listen to us," she said. I felt kind of sad for her. It was true. People didn't listen to old people. Old people and children.

Mrs. Stein opened a little book like the ones we used at our Shabbat meals. By now I knew it was called a *bentcher*. It contained the blessing you have to say after eating bread.

"Excuse me for a minute while I *bentch*," she said.

While we waited, I looked around the dining room. Except for a man a few tables away, also *bentching*, the room was empty. He had a bushy, white beard and wore a black *kippa*. He rocked back and forth as he said the blessing.

"I don't think I've seen him before," Rebecca whispered. "Maybe he's new and would like someone to talk to."

"I don't know," I said hesitantly. I couldn't imagine what we'd have to say to each other.

"Just tell him you're with the *Mitzvah* Project. Then start asking him questions."

"Like what?"

"Like where he's from, does he have children, does he like it here. It's much easier than you think."

I wasn't sure about that.

"It's a *mitzvah*," Rebecca said coaxingly.

"Okay, okay," I finally said, only half-convinced.

"He may be old, but he won't bite," Mrs. Stein said, winking at me. I wasn't so sure about that, either.

Just as I got to his table the old man put away his *bentcher*. I stood there for a few moments, not knowing what to say. He straightened his suspenders and put on a worn-looking black jacket, without acknowledging me. Finally, he looked up from where he sat. He stared at me and I stared at him, but neither of us said anything. I started to feel kind of itchy all over; that happened to me sometimes when I was nervous. I could hear a voice inside my head telling me to think of something to say, but I kept drawing a blank.

"So...what is it?" the old man finally said kind of gruffly, breaking the silence. He had a very thick accent.

"I, I...um...hi, my name is Libby. Libby Ross," I finally blurted out. I could be such an idiot sometimes. After all, he really wasn't going to bite me. I ran on nervously, telling him all about the *Mitzvah* Project, looking down at the floor the whole time. There, I'd gotten it all out. I sighed with relief and looked up at him. He was squinting his eyes and pursing his lips. Maybe he did bite. I scratched myself under my chin.

"I don't mean I should insult you, Miss Ross," he began when I finished. "But I don't want you should waste your time with me. I'm sure you have better things to do with your time and so do I. I don't belong in this place. I won't be here long."

I knew it. Now what was I supposed to say? I glanced at Rebecca. She and Mrs. Stein were talking and paying no attention to me. I looked back at the old man. He didn't want some young do-gooder treating him like a charity case. He started to stand up. I didn't know what to say except what I was really thinking.

"I can't blame you for not wanting to be here. It smells bad and it's dark and depressing. I don't know why they call it a retirement 'home.' It feels more like a prison to me," I said all in one breath.

The old man looked at me and sat back down. I thought I saw a small smile forming at one corner of his mouth. He still didn't say anything, but he seemed to be listening so I went on, not really sure what would come out of my mouth next.

"I don't really go to school with these girls, and I'm not like them. Rebecca, she's over there, we're friends and I spent the night with her. She's my only friend here. You see, I just moved in. This is my first Shabbat ever."

"Your first Shabbat? You never before kept Shabbos?" the old man asked, his voice softening a bit.

"Nope. My parents don't do anything Jewish."

"I see. So what do you think? You like Shabbat?"

"Yeah...most of it, anyway. I mean, there's an awful lot of things you're not allowed to do, and I don't know if I like that." Then I told him about the stuff I did like. Like the candles and the food, and singing songs after dinner. I told him about how I'd met Rebecca and about how nice her family was. Before long I was talking about my family. About how my parents were so busy that I hardly ever saw them, and about seeing Sheila driving with her friends and how we were always fighting, and about having a maid, and missing Connecticut. I went on and on until the old man cleared his throat and I realized I had been telling him all about myself. It was supposed to be the other way around. I could feel my face turning all red. I stopped talking and looked at him. He smiled at me.

"I'm not very good at this, I guess. Rebecca said I was supposed to get you to talk. I'll go now if you want me to." I started to get up.

"No, wait," the old man said. He smiled at me for the first time, revealing a missing front tooth. "I have a feeling we could both use a friend, no?" he said.

We stared at each other as I thought about it for a moment. I kind of liked this old man. For some reason he was easy to talk to. He really seemed to listen to me. "Yeah, I guess so," I finally said.

He grinned again and hit the table. "Good. My name is Mr. Goldblum. It's a pleasure to meet you," he said, as if we were only just meeting.

I smiled back at Mr. Goldblum, and he told me to have a seat. Now I started asking him questions about himself, like I was supposed to. He answered, then asked me more stuff about myself, as if he really were interested. Pretty soon we were getting to know all about one another. The time passed so quickly, I didn't even notice the hour was over and Rebecca was calling for me to leave. Mr. Goldblum asked me to come again next Shabbat and I promised I would.

"Well, how did it go?" Rebecca asked as we opened the front door and stepped out into the bright day.

I took a deep breath of fresh air. I thought of my conversation with Mr. Goldblum. I'd told him all about my troubles and he really listened and seemed to understand. He'd said I reminded him of his daughter, Katrina. I thought of how sad he had looked when he spoke of her. His eyes had filled with tears. He told me she was only my age when she had died in a place called Auschwitz during World War II. Mr. Goldblum couldn't believe I'd never heard of Auschwitz. He was just going to tell me about it when Rebecca called for me. I'd have to wait until next week to find out more. How awful to die so young. Poor Katrina. But especially, poor Mr. Goldblum.

"Libby?" Rebecca said, waiting for a response.

"You were right. I think Mr. Goldblum could use a friend like me," I answered Rebecca. And I had a hunch that I could use a friend like him, too.

Chapter 8

I was the last one up on Sunday morning, and found everybody in the kitchen eating breakfast. Except for Dad. As usual, he was still sleeping. He always slept late on Sundays, then went to the office for a few hours to "catch up." Sometimes it seemed like he spent his whole life just catching up.

"Good morning," Mom greeted me, glancing up from the newspaper.

"Hi," I said, walking over to the cupboard to get a cereal bowl.

"Shh, honey, not so loud," my mother said to Mandy, who was banging her spoon on her tray and singing some nonsensical song. She stopped for a moment and looked at my mother, as if deciding whether or not to listen.

"Libby! Libby!" she said, holding her arms out to me.

I went over to her and gave her a hug.

Sheila peeked out from behind three different kinds of cereal boxes. "Where have you been?" she asked in between big bites.

"At Rebecca's."

"Oh yeah, I forgot....Hey, does she have any older brothers?"

"No, she doesn't have any older brothers," I said, mimicking her voice. That was so typical. All she ever thought about was boys, boys, boys. I sat down next to her with my box of Cheerios. "That is so gross," I said, looking at the mound of cereal mixtures in her bowl.

"You have no taste," Sheila replied. She proceeded to shove a huge spoonful into her mouth, chew it up, then open her mouth to show me what was inside. I cringed and looked the other way.

Mandy started banging her spoon and singing again. Mom called Quana in and told her to get Mandy dressed. She started to cry when Quana lifted her out of the highchair. Sometimes I felt like Mandy was being gypped or something. At least when I was a baby, Mom was still taking care of us. I wondered if Mandy knew the difference. I mean, she really liked Quana and everything. But a mom's a mom and no one can replace her.

When things settled down again, I started to tell Mom about Rebecca. As I went on about lighting the candles and saying all the blessings, and about how I'd accidentally turned on the light, I noticed the expression on my mom's face change. She looked concerned, like she had the other night when she'd almost changed her mind about letting me go. Finally she interrupted me. "Aren't there any kids you'd like to invite over from your music class?" she asked.

"Why? What's wrong with Rebecca?" I wanted to know, still confused as ever by this strange reaction.

My mother didn't answer right away. "Nothing," she finally said. "Well actually..." she paused again and looked exasperated. "I just thought it would be nice for you to have other friends, too."

"But I like Rebecca," I insisted. "And she likes me. Besides, the other girls aren't interested in the new kid in town."

"Well, that's because they don't know you," Mom said, trying to make me feel better. "Try inviting one of them over for a swim. Once you've made friends with one of them, the others will follow."

"When you're new you have to go out of your way a little bit. You can't just wait around for them to make the first move, you know," Sheila butted in. I shot her a glance, knowing very well what she was doing to be accepted. Then again, at least she was making friends, which was more than I could say for myself...except, of course, for Rebecca. I took a spoonful of my cereal instead of answering. Mom didn't understand. And neither did I, for that matter. What was wrong with Rebecca? But finally I said I'd try to make other friends. After all, how else would I get Mom to allow me to go over to Rebecca's again next Friday night?

*   *   *

Later I asked Mom if I could go to the library. I didn't tell her, but I wanted to find some books on Judaism. She asked me to take Mandy along and check out some books for her. On the way out, we passed my dad in his usual Sunday spot: the big leather recliner in the den. He was reading the *Wall Street Journal* and listening to an opera.

"Bye, Dad," I said. He looked up over his paper and smiled at us. Mandy ran over to him and he lifted her onto his lap.

"Where have you been all weekend?" he asked me.

"I slept over at my friend Rebecca's," I said, careful not to mention anything about Shabbat.

"I'm glad to see you're making friends. California isn't so bad after all, is it?"

"It's okay. But I'd still rather be in Connecticut."

"You don't know how lucky you are. Most people only dream of living such a good life."

I could have said a few things about that, but he had already handed Mandy back to me and returned to his paper. Maybe I *was* lucky compared to a lot of people, I thought as we headed out. Certainly, I was luckier than the ice cream store bag lady or the old people forced to live in the Golden Years Retirement Home. We did have a lot of nice stuff. But I couldn't help thinking of the Kleins. All six of them lived in a small duplex and somehow they seemed to have all they needed. I think I would have traded my own room, the swimming pool, and the grand piano just to have my father spend Friday nights with us.

*   *   *

Rebecca called on Wednesday night to see if I was coming for Shabbat. I told her I'd have to ask my mom when she was preoccupied with her writing so she'd be sure to say yes. Later that night, I heard her computer going so I peeked into her room and got the answer I wanted. For once I was glad she was so busy writing.

I got into bed and continued reading the book the librarian had given me. I usually don't like history books, but this one was really interesting. It was incredible how the Jewish people had survived after all the suffering we'd been through. All throughout history there'd always been some group of people who'd hated us and tried to destroy us. It was hard to believe that the people the book was talking about were actually my ancestors, that I was part of the Jewish people. These weren't just fairy tales. The book said it was our traditions, customs, and belief in one God that had helped us survive. I'd never cared before about being Jewish. I mean, it had never made a difference to me. But now, as I learned more and more, I was starting to care. I kind of liked it, in fact. That's why I couldn't understand why my parents had never taught us anything about it.

*   *   *

On Friday afternoon I dressed up for Shabbat.
I chose my favorite purple and yellow flowered
skirt and white and yellow striped blouse. Then I
picked the biggest and prettiest roses I could find
for the Shabbat table. Mrs. Klein couldn't believe
they were from our very own garden. I felt more
comfortable this time because at least I'd seen it all
before. Besides, they all made me feel so at home. I
soon forgot about being shy and found myself asking
a bunch of questions at dinner. Like why is it a
mitzvah for a woman to cover her hair?

"Because it's *tznius!*" Sarah proclaimed loudly.

"*Tznius* means modesty," Rebecca explained. "Once
you get married your husband is the only man
who's allowed to see your hair."

"You're kidding."

"No," Rebecca said, shaking her head.

"But why?" I asked.

Rebecca thought for a moment while Mrs. Klein
passed some chicken and potato kugel my way.
"Because walking around with your hair uncovered
is like walking around in pants or a mini-skirt. It's
immodest."

"You mean you never wear pants?" I asked in
disbelief.

Rebecca blushed and looked to her mother for
help.

"We try to choose clothes that don't draw too
much attention to our bodies," Mrs. Klein explained.

"But I always wear pants," I said a little defensively. I didn't see what was so immodest about that. I mean, the whole world wore pants, so what was the big deal?

Mrs. Klein continued, "If you've always dressed a certain way it doesn't seem so immodest to you. But if I walked out of the house in pants or without my hair covered, I'd feel like I was practically undressed."

Sarah giggled.

It was hard to believe that they even had laws about how to dress. "They?" I guess I meant "we." After all, I was Jewish, too. But their world was so different from mine. I wasn't doing any of this stuff. So what, I began to wonder, made me Jewish?

We continued to talk about this strange *tznius* business. "If we can be modest on the outside, it will lead to inner modesty," Mrs. Klein said.

I wasn't exactly sure what she meant by that, but if she was an example of *tznius* then I kind of had an idea. She did seem very modest. She always spoke so quietly and politely. She didn't yell and get all excited when she wanted people to listen, like I sometimes did. But it wasn't like she was a wimp, either. She could be very firm when she needed to be. I'd seen her be that way with us kids. And I could tell Mr. Klein really respected her by the way he looked at her and listened when she talked. I really respected her, too.

"Besides, it's a constant reminder that God is above me," Mrs. Klein said, looking up at the ceiling. "And I constantly need to be reminded."

I was glad when Mr. Klein broke into a song. I

had enough to think about for a week. Rebecca and I helped clear the table and bring out dessert. It was a peach pie. Sarah sang along with Mr. Klein and Chana banged her spoon on her tray, saying, "Pie! Pie!"

I ate my pie in quiet thought as the singing filled the room. There was a lot that seemed strange to me, and I certainly didn't understand it all, or even agree with everything. But there was something about Shabbat that, well...just felt right. Like when you hear your parents get home late at night and you listen from your bed as they check all the doors, and you know everything is as it should be. As I sat there, I realized I was feeling sort of sad that I'd missed out on Shabbat all these years. Like I'd been gypped or something. I wished this night could go on forever. Then I remembered it would come again next week and every week after that! And there was still tomorrow's lunch and visiting Mr. Goldblum. I had been thinking about him a lot and was especially anxious to find out more about his daughter, Katrina, and Auschwitz. I hoped he remembered I was coming, and that he hadn't changed his mind about wanting to be friends.

Chapter 9

WHEN I arrived at the retirement home, Mr. Goldblum was nowhere to be seen. Finally one of the nurses told me he had hurt his back and was upstairs in bed.

"I don't think he's up to visitors today," she said.

"But I know he'll want to see me," I insisted.

"I'm sorry, Miss, he needs his rest. Come back next week."

I knew if I didn't see him, he might think I'd forgotten or changed my mind. Besides, the nurse didn't know what she was talking about. I knew how I felt when I had to stay in bed. That was when you wanted visitors the most. I waited for the nurse to get busy with some of the other residents, then quickly turned the corner that led to the private rooms. It took a while to find him, but finally I peeked into a room and found Mr. Goldblum lying on his back. He was sleeping with his mouth open and making a lot of noise as he breathed. I didn't think I should wake him so I sat down in a chair by his bed and waited a little while, hoping he'd wake up soon. As I sat there I looked around his little room. There wasn't much to look at. Just a chair with clothes piled on top of it, an old dresser, a mirror that distorted you when you looked into it, and the ugliest painting I ever saw of the sea on a stormy day. It was the kind of painting you see for sale on the sidewalk. At least they could have picked one with the sun shining. I felt bad thinking of Mr. Goldblum spending so much of his time here.

There were a few photographs on his dresser and I walked over to look at them. One was a picture of Mr. Goldblum when he was a lot younger. He wore a black hat and his beard hadn't yet turned gray. He was standing next to a woman with a scarf on her head. I held the picture up and looked closer. She was pretty. I guessed her to be Mr. Goldblum's wife. He hadn't mentioned his wife before, and I wondered where she was. Sitting beside that was an old black and white picture of a girl who looked about my age. Her hair was in two braids and she had a big smile on her face, just like Mr. Goldblum's. She looked a lot like him. I knew this was Katrina. She looked like someone I would have liked to have for a friend.

I moved over to the mirror and held her picture next to my face. I could see why I reminded Mr. Goldblum of her. We both had curly hair and freckles. I wondered what I'd look like in braids and decided to try it out. I found two worn rubber bands on Mr. Goldblum's dresser and finished off the braids just as I heard him stir. I looked at myself in the mirror—I kind of liked the way it looked. Then I turned towards Mr. Goldblum to say hello.

He opened his eyes and a big smile came over his face. "Katrina," he said.

Oh no, what had I done? "Mr. Goldblum, it's me, Libby...Libby Ross."

"Libby?" he said as if he didn't remember me. His smile disappeared.

I quickly moved in closer so he could get a better look. I took his hand in mine. "I wanted to see how I'd look in braids. Like your daughter in the picture," I continued.

Mr. Goldblum took a good look at me and slowly sat himself up in bed. Finally he smiled again. "It suits you well, Libby," he said. I sighed with relief and helped prop him up better, until he seemed more comfortable.

"When you get old sometimes your mind can fool you," Mr. Goldblum began. "You can't always tell the difference between what's in here," he said, pointing to his head, "and what's real. For a moment I thought you were my daughter, Katrina. My eyes are not so good anymore and my mind plays games with me."

"I'm sorry, Mr. Goldblum. I didn't mean to confuse you," I apologized.

"Don't be sorry, *maidelah*. I'm happy it's you. Do you know what that means, '*maidelah*'?" he asked.

I shook my head no.

"It means little girl, but when we say it we

mean it affectionately. That's what I used to call Katrina. I may call you that, no?"

"I guess so," I said. It was a little weird-sounding, but why not? If it would make him happy. That's what this *Mitzvah* Project was all about, wasn't it?

"Do they know you are here with me?" he asked.

"Not exactly," I said. "There's this fat nurse who said—"

"I know, I know. You'd think I were a small child the way they treat me sometimes," Mr. Goldblum interrupted. He sighed and the smile left his face again as if he were in pain.

"How did you hurt your back?" I asked.

"I was catching myself from a fall."

"You fell down?!"

"Not to worry, not to worry. It happens when you get older. I'll be back on my feet in no time. You will see." Mr. Goldblum smiled and clapped his hands as if to change the subject. "Now, enough about me. What shall we talk about today, eh?"

I reminded Mr. Goldblum about the discussion we'd had last week, and how we'd been interrupted and where he'd left off. I asked again about Auschwitz.

Mr. Goldblum took a deep breath. "Ah, I see you did not forget. That is good to have a curious mind." He closed his eyes and shifted his position again. I could see he was distressed. "Two generations and already they have forgotten," he said, more to himself than to me. He moved around some more, still trying to find a comfortable position. I asked him if he was all right.

"A little backache isn't going to kill me," he said as he managed to smile at me. "This is good," he continued. "It's good that I should tell you about Auschwitz. So you should tell your children and they should tell their children and nobody should ever forget." But just then the nurse I had seen downstairs suddenly appeared in the doorway.

"Young lady, I thought I told you Mr. Goldblum wasn't receiving visitors today," she said.

"Mr. Goldblum is feeling much better since his visitor came," Mr. Goldblum said, winking at me.

"Well it's time for your shot," she said, holding up a needle. "I'll have to ask you to leave," she said to me.

I looked at Mr. Goldblum and he winked at me again. "She was just leaving, Miss Stone." Then he said to me, "Now Libby, I want you should do something. Go to the library and get a book called *The Diary of Anne Frank*. I think you will enjoy reading it. Then next time you come we will talk about Auschwitz."

"Okay," I said as Miss Stone squeezed her way past me.

"Okay, let's turn you over, Mr. Goldblum," she said as if he were two years old. Then she turned around and looked at me. "Goodbye, young lady," she said. As I left I stiffened my face to imitate the nurse's and Mr. Goldblum chuckled. I was glad I could make him laugh.

Chapter 10

THE next Shabbat I had to stay home because the Kleins were spending it with friends in another part of town. It was late Friday afternoon, and I was sitting outside our house imagining what I'd be doing if I had been at Rebecca's.

"Libby! Hi, Libby!" Quana came out carrying Mandy, and asked me to watch her while she fixed dinner. Mandy spotted a steady stream of ants carrying crumbs to their anthill and started to laugh and jump up and down on top of them. I had problems, all right, but at least I hadn't been born an ant!

"What's for dinner?" I asked Quana.

"Enchiladas," she said. She pointed to Mandy and laughed, then went back inside.

Maybe it was because my mind was on Shabbat and I was thinking of what I'd be doing if I had been at the Kleins. But for the first time since moving it occurred to me that Quana might like some help in the kitchen. Sure, she was paid to cook and clean. But this was my house and we were a family and that meant that everyone should chip in, didn't it? That's the way the Kleins did it. And anyway, I was curious about how to make an enchilada.

Quana was surprised when I said I wanted to help, but she went along with me. It turned out to be a lot of fun for all of us. She taught me how to fry tortillas, then fill them with cheese and sauce. Mandy helped by tearing lettuce for the salad. As we worked, Quana turned on the radio to one of the Spanish stations and started to sing along. I imitated her in my best Spanish accent and danced around the kitchen. Quana laughed and tickled me. There we were, frying tortillas and dancing to mariachi music in our own kitchen. It made me think for the first time about how Quana had a whole life of her own that I didn't know anything about. She had a family in Mexico whom she sent money home to every month. She had her own language and her own kinds of food and music, and I bet she got real homesick being away from everything she loved so much. Kind of like I felt not being able to have Shabbat. That's when it occurred to me that if you can't be in Mexico, you bring Mexico to America. Like Quana. She still ate her kind of food and listened to her own music. She did the best she could to bring her real home into our house. Couldn't I do the same thing?

I glanced at the clock. There was still some time before the sun went down. Where could I get some *challah*? I looked in the freezer. There was a loaf of French bread. It wasn't freshly baked *chal-lah*, but it would do. I could set the table with our good dishes and pick flowers from our yard for a centerpiece. I found a bottle of grape juice to use for *Kiddush*, even if I didn't know the blessing. But I had learned "*Hamotzi*" by now and could say that over the bread. I found some candles and candle-sticks in the china cabinet and brought them to my room. I knew just where to put them: on the ledge by my big window, where I could watch them burn as I lay in bed at night. My father would be meet-ing my mother for dinner like he always did on Friday nights, so I knew I didn't have to worry about them. Sheila would probably be out with friends, so it would just be Quana, Mandy, and I. I could teach Quana a Shabbat song. It would be fun!

I showered and put on one of my good dresses, then got Mandy into her party dress and patent leather shoes. She loved getting all dressed up.

"Party?" she asked.

"Well sort of. We're having our own little party right here. It's called Shabbat."

"Sabbat, Sabbat," Mandy tried to say it.

Quana's English wasn't very good and I didn't know any Spanish, so I tried my best to explain it to her.

"It's what Jewish people like us celebrate on Friday night with a special dinner. On Saturday we go to the synagogue to pray. Then we come back and have another big family meal together."

"Ah, *sí*! The Sabbath. Pour us on Sundays. Pour

you Saturday. *Si, si*," she said.

She did understand. Quana was Catholic. She went to church on Sundays like we went to shul on Saturdays.

"So tonight we're going to have a special Shabbat dinner."

"*Si, si*...okay," she said, smiling at me.

When it was time to light the candles, I brought Quana and Mandy into my room and turned off my light. "We light candles right before the sun goes down, to welcome Shabbat," I said.

"Candles!" Mandy cried, happily clapping her hands.

Just like I'd learned at Rebecca's, I lit the candles, covered my eyes, and said the blessing out loud.

"*Moui bonita*," Quana said. "Very pretty."

"Bonita! Bonita!" Mandy imitated.

The sky was growing darker by the minute, and the two little candles burning in my window lit up the whole room. It really did look beautiful. We were all so engrossed in the moment, none of us even heard my father get home. The sound of his voice took me completely by surprise and I jumped.

"What are you doing, Libby?" His voice seemed to rock the peaceful room.

"Dad!" I cried out, turning around. "I didn't hear you come in."

"Apparently not," he said. The expression on his face was not a happy one.

"I thought you were meeting Mom for dinner," I said.

"Daddy!" Mandy cried, running to him. My father

lifted her up, kissed her quickly, then handed her to Quana.

"Quana, give Mandy some dinner," he ordered abruptly. Why was he so upset?

Quana carried Mandy out, leaving me alone with my father. "Where did you learn how to do that?" he demanded as he walked into my room.

"It isn't hard to light candles," I said, knowing that wasn't what he meant.

"You know what I mean, Libby. I was standing here watching you. I heard you say the blessing." He walked over to the candles and blew them out. I looked back and forth from him to the smoldering wicks. I could feel a lump growing in my throat.

"Answer me!" he said sternly.

"From Rebecca," I whispered.

"What's going on here?" my mother said, entering my room with a stack of books from the library.

"Doris, do you know anything at all about this Rebecca friend Libby's been spending so much time with?"

My mother put down the books and rubbed her eyes. "I just got home, Irv. Can we talk about this later?"

"No, we can't."

My mother leaned against my desk. "Okay, what's the problem?"

That's exactly what I wanted to know.

"Have you ever met her?" my father demanded.

"Why should you suddenly be so interested in who Libby's friends are, Irv? It's never mattered before." I could tell my mom was trying to sidestep the issue.

"This is different. You know it is," my father said.

"Why is this different?" I asked, but Dad ignored me.

"If you were ever around enough to see what's going on with your children, it might have occurred to you that this move has been very difficult for Libby," my mother said.

"Don't start on me, Doris," my father said, standing up.

"Well then don't *you* start on *me*. I was pleased Libby had made a friend. She was moping around the house for days with nobody to play with and—"

"And this was a convenient way to get her out of your hair so you didn't have to entertain her," my father interrupted.

My parents really knew how to make a person feel loved. They were at it again...as if I weren't there.

"You know how I feel about this, Doris!"

"Well, I can't be watching over them every minute and screening every friend. If it's so important to you, you find the time!" my mother yelled.

"That's not my job! You're the mother!" my father yelled back. Their voices were getting louder and louder.

"And since when have fathers been exempted from responsibility for their children?" my mother lashed out.

"Okay, fine. I'll stay home and raise the kids and you go out and make a living for us!"

"What do you think my writing is all about?"

my mother demanded.

"Your children come first!"

"They're your children, too!"

This was getting unbearable. "Stop it!" I finally yelled at the top of my lungs.

My parents shut up for a minute. They both looked at me, then back at each other. My mother took a deep breath to calm herself down. "I didn't see the harm in letting Libby spend a few Friday nights with her new friend. You know how she loves sleepovers."

"I don't think they're just ordinary sleepovers. You don't know about people like this," my father said, trying to stay cool.

"People like what?" I asked. But nobody listened.

"My God, Irv. You make it sound as if they're teaching her to murder or something. Kids will be kids. They like to play with candles."

"She was saying the blessing in Hebrew. She wasn't just playing."

My dad was right about that.

"I think you're really overreacting, Irv."

"You know how I feel about this," my father said again. Then he turned to me. I was still sitting on my bed, holding my Raggedy Ann, trying to smooth out the tangles in her hair.

"I better not find you doing this again. Do you hear me?" my father said sharply.

I was only sitting two feet away. What did he think?

"And you're not going to have any more of these so-called Friday-night sleepovers at this new friend of yours, either," he concluded.

Before I could even protest he left my room.

"But Mom!" I started.

"Not now, Libby," she snapped, then followed my father.

Not now?! So when? They acted like I didn't have any say in this matter, like I was just a...a Raggedy Ann doll. Maybe I'd be better off if I were. Then I remembered the table and ran to the kitchen to put everything away before my dad saw it. Quana and Mandy were eating.

"Sabbat?" Mandy said.

"Not tonight. Not in this house, anyway."

Later that night, as I sat in my room, I could hear my parents arguing. If only I could make out their words. Then I heard Sheila come home with a few of her new friends. They all went into the bathroom and spent a few hundred hours doing something in there. When they came out, Sheila popped her head into my room. I couldn't believe my eyes! She'd bleached her hair so blond, it was practically white! Her face was all made up like some fashion model, and big, dangly earrings hung practically down to her shoulders. Her two girlfriends came out of the bathroom and stood behind Sheila in the doorway, giggling. They all looked the same.

"Well, how do we look?" Sheila asked.

I hardly recognized her. I didn't like it at all and just stared at her without saying anything.

"Well?" she asked again, striking a model pose and pursing her lips. Her friends did the same thing and they all giggled some more.

"Wow," I finally managed to say. I didn't want

to tell her what I was really thinking. I wasn't sure why, but it really bothered me, her acting this way. It all seemed so...I don't know, phoney.

"Has Mom seen you?" I asked.

"It's my hair. I can do what I want with it," Sheila said defensively.

We both knew that wasn't true. I could just imagine the scene later when my mother found out. (Actually, there was a scene, but somehow Sheila managed to convince my mother that all of her friends' mothers were letting them do it, and Mom just let it go. Why couldn't she be as easy on me?)

"Hey, we could dye Libby's hair," one of her friends suggested.

"And straighten it, too," the other one said.

"Yeah, how 'bout it, Lib?" Sheila joined in. "You could use a make-over."

"Thanks a lot. But no thanks," I said.

"Well, how about a little makeup, then? You know, you really should care a little more about what you look like," Sheila persisted.

"I'm not allowed to wear makeup yet," I reminded her.

"Oh, you're no fun. I'm just trying to be helpful. Come on, you guys, let's go," Sheila said, leading her friends to her room. In a minute loud rock 'n' roll music was blasting through her closed door.

I looked at the blown-out candles in my window. Then I closed my eyes and imagined the Kleins' living room with all the candles neatly lined up, burning in the darkened room. Tears welled up in my eyes.

Chapter 11

I began to read *The Diary of Anne Frank* that weekend. It was hard to believe it was a true story. Just like Mr. Goldblum's daughter, Katrina, Anne Frank was once a real little girl like me. She lived in the 1940s, during World War II, when Hitler had tried to exterminate all the Jews. She was a few years older than I at the time. For a few years, she lived hidden away in a small attic above her father's offices. The entrance was disguised by a secret door built to look like a bookcase. They weren't allowed to go outside for two years. The only glimpse she had of the world was what she saw through a little window in the attic. She lived in constant fear of being discovered and killed or taken away to a concentration camp. I found out that Auschwitz was the name of one of those camps.

I learned that the Nazis despised the Jewish people. They robbed them of everything they owned and sent them to the camps. These were horrible,

horrible places where the Jews were forced to do hard labor out in the freezing cold, without proper clothes or shoes. Many starved to death or died of disease. Everyone else was killed. And for no reason other than being Jewish. I'd learned a little about Hitler and the Nazis in school, but never in much detail. Why hadn't they taught us more? Why had the Nazis hated us so much?

Saturday night I woke up in a cold sweat. I'd dreamt that Hitler was alive and he came to our house to take us all away. My father kept yelling, "We're not Jewish!" But Hitler's henchmen didn't believe him and they finally shot him. I changed into another nightgown, then tiptoed into Mandy's room and lifted her out of her crib. Just smelling her and feeling her warm body made me feel better. I brought her into my bed with me and finally fell asleep again.

The next morning, Mandy and I were sitting down to eat some Cheerios and toast when the doorbell rang. But before I could even get up to get it, I heard a key turn in the door and somebody enter.

"Hello? Isn't anybody up yet?" It was Abby. Now she had a key to our house. Next thing you know, she'd be moving in, and probably into my room! She jogged into the kitchen wearing a pink sweatsuit, pink running shoes, and a pink sweatband around her forehead. It was enough to make me never want to wear pink again.

"Hi, kids. Oh how nice, getting your baby sister breakfast," she said to me as she kissed Mandy. What a phoney.

Abby proceeded to make a pot of coffee. "Your mom's not up yet? I told her I'd be here early. We have a lot of work to do. Libby, honey, why don't you go tell her I'm here?"

"You want me to wake her up?" My mom hated us to wake her up on weekend mornings.

"She's expecting me, love. She probably slept through her alarm."

On second thought I decided it wasn't such a bad idea. It would give me a chance to talk to her about last night before she got busy writing. But just as I got up, Mom entered the kitchen, rubbing her eyes sleepily. She was dressed in a worn pair of gray sweatpants and one of my dad's big sweatshirts.

"You weren't kidding," she said to Abby.

"Rise and shine, honey. You'll feel better after the run."

Mom moaned.

Abby started to do leg stretches. "A healthy body makes a healthy mind. And it wouldn't hurt to get yourself a decent tracksuit, either."

My mom looked down at her outfit, then at Abby's. I liked hers a lot better.

"Mommy," Mandy said, reaching out to my mom. Mom lifted her up, then started to pour herself a cup of coffee.

"Uh, uh," Abby scolded, taking the cup from her. "After we run." My mom groaned again and put Mandy back in her high chair. Mandy started to whimper.

"Mommy has to exercise," Mom said, kissing

Mandy and taking a bite of her toast. Abby took Mom's arm and led her out of the kitchen.

"You have to learn to shut it out, honey," I heard her say as they left. I could have socked her in the face. I jumped out of my seat and chased after my mom.

"But Mom, what about last night?"

"We'll talk later, Libby," she said, still being pulled by Abby.

"It's always 'later.' But 'later' never comes," I complained as Abby opened the front door and ushered Mom through.

"I have a lot to do today. We'll talk at dinner. I promise," she said as the door slammed in my face. I'd heard that before.

I went back to the kitchen and, for some reason, the first thing I noticed was Abby's purse. It was sitting on the counter by the coffee pot. I certainly hadn't planned to do it again. In fact, quite the contrary, I was going to return the money. But I was so fed up with Abby and so angry at my mother that, without thinking, I pulled out Abby's wallet and took another ten-dollar bill. She'd never miss it and I could think of a million things to do with it. Like give some to the bag lady, and maybe even buy something pretty for Mr. Goldblum to hang on his wall. That thought made me feel better about taking more money. After all, it was for a good cause.

Mandy was still crying so I went over to her and picked her up. She started calling for Quana so I took her into Quana's room. She was already up ironing some clothes, singing along with the radio. I put Mandy down on the floor, then sat down next to her. Quana sensed that I was unhappy about something and got down on the floor and tickled me until I laughed. Then we both started playing around with Mandy. Quana was all right.

Chapter 12

WHEN my mom got back I asked her if I could go to the library. I was really planning to visit Mr. Goldblum, so when she told me to take Mandy along I started to protest. It didn't do any good. Oh well...I wasn't going to let that stop me.

I buckled Mandy into my bike basket and rode as fast as I could. Mandy squealed happily.

"Come on, Mandy. Let's get some ice cream."

"Ice cream! Ice cream!" she chanted as I crossed the street and parked my bike. This time I didn't hesitate when I saw the bag lady in front of the ice cream store. I stopped in front of her and reached into my pocket. Then I realized I only had a ten-dollar bill, no change. She was looking at me, waiting. "Hi, lady!" Mandy suddenly blurted out. She smiled at Mandy, revealing a mouth full of rotten teeth.

"Kootchy koo!" she said, reaching out and tickling Mandy in the tummy. "Name's Berthenia," she announced, straightening up. "What's yours?"

"Libby," I said softly, not sure if I should be giving her this information.

"And hers?" she asked, pointing to Mandy.

"Mandy," I said.

"Mandy? Rhymes with candy. Ha! Mandy want some candy?"

"Candy! Candy!" Mandy cried, jumping up and down.

The lady reached into the pocket of her ragged sweater, brought out a piece of candy, and handed it to Mandy. I didn't want Mandy to eat it because it looked old and dirty, but I didn't want to offend Berthenia either.

"Thank you," I said quickly. "Come on, Mandy, let's get some ice cream." I was thinking that I'd give Berthenia some change when we came back out, but then I realized she might be hungry so I asked her if she'd like ice cream.

"Chocolate ripple," she said without a pause. "But they won't let me in."

"I'll be right back," I said.

"Ripple rhymes with triple. I'd like a triple ripple!" I heard her call after us. She was pretty kooky.

I took the candy away from Mandy when we got into the store and she started to cry. But once she saw all the ice cream she stopped. When I asked for two single chocolate ripple cones and one triple, the man behind the counter looked back and forth from me to Berthenia.

"She bothering you?" he asked.

"No, sir."

"Can't keep her away from here."

"I don't think she's hurting anyone," I said.

The man rolled his eyes.

Once outside, I gave Berthenia the cone, then handed her a few dollars.

"God bless you, child!" she declared, taking a huge bite of ice cream.

"Well, we have to go now," I said, buckling Mandy into the basket. But Berthenia was so busy eating her ice cream that she didn't even bother to say goodbye. Oh well, she may have been a crazy old bag lady, but she was funny and I kind of liked her. I rode off feeling all warm and tingly inside. There really was something about doing a *mitzvah*.

At the retirement home, I found Mr. Goldblum sitting with Rebecca's friend, Mrs. Stein. So he'd made a new friend! They were both real happy to see me and made a big fuss over Mandy.

"How's your back?" I asked.

"Much better. I told you it wouldn't be so long." I was glad when Mrs. Stein took Mandy to meet her other friends. It would give me time alone with Mr. Goldblum.

"So tell me, what's new since last I saw you?" Mr. Goldblum asked when we were alone.

Just his asking stirred up all of my emotions again and a lump swelled in my throat. I swallowed real hard and struggled to fight back tears. "I just wanted to have Shabbat since I couldn't go to Rebecca's. I mean, what's so bad about lighting a few candles?" I bit my lip, but the tears came anyway.

"Why don't you start from the beginning?" Mr. Goldblum suggested, handing me a handkerchief.

So I did. I told him everything. And he listened without interrupting even once.

"You must try talking to your father," he said when I finally stopped talking.

I told him it wouldn't do any good.

"You must never give up before you try."

"But he doesn't listen to me. Believe me," I insisted.

"I believe you, *maidelah*. But I was once a father, so you must listen to me. You must ask him why he acts this way."

"I heard my mother say there are skeletons in the closet. What does that mean?" I asked, thinking of a conversation I'd heard between my mother and Abby.

"Ah...it means there are, how shall I say...secrets."

"Oh. Well, that's for sure. I just wish I knew what they were," I said.

"There is always hope. You must approach your father at the right time, when he is not busy or with work on his mind."

"Ha. That's never," I informed him.

"Please promise me you will try."

Maybe there was something to what Mr. Goldblum was saying. Maybe it would be best to speak with my father directly, instead of with Mom. After all, he was the one with all the objections. "Okay," I halfheartedly agreed. "I'll try."

"That's my girl," Mr. Goldblum said, smiling at me. "Ah...I see your sister's a big hit." We looked over as a small circle of old people gathered around Mandy. She was loving all the attention. Good. There was still a lot I wanted to talk about.

I told Mr. Goldblum that I'd been reading *The Diary of Anne Frank* and that now I knew Auschwitz was a concentration camp where thousands and thousands of Jews had died during World War II. I asked him if he and his wife had also been there. I watched as Mr. Goldblum's expression changed. He looked away from me and stared out the window across the room. He seemed to forget I was there for a few moments. I cleared my throat to get his attention. Finally he looked back at me and took a deep breath.

"No, I was at another camp called Treblinka. My wife was with Katrina."

"You mean she died there, too?"

"No, *maidelah*. Thank God, she survived the camp. We later had many happy years together. She died five years ago."

"But why didn't you have more children, then?"

Mr. Goldblum told me they had tried and tried but the camps had left his wife too weak and sickly. I couldn't imagine anything more awful than what Mr. Goldblum had been through. How could God let that happen to anyone?

"Ah, the million-dollar question," he said, taking another deep breath. "I can only tell you how I see it," he began. "God gives each and every one of us the ability to choose good or to choose bad. Hitler chose bad. And many other people, the people who made up his armies, chose bad. The bad became very big and powerful."

"More powerful than God?" I asked.

"Nothing is more powerful than God."

"Then why didn't God stop the bad?"

"He did. Eventually." Mr. Goldblum took out his handkerchief and wiped little beads of sweat off his face.

"But why did it take so long? Why did Katrina have to die?"

Mr. Goldblum's eyes became watery. I hadn't wanted to upset him. I could tell it was time to stop talking about it. I said I was sorry for making him sad.

"You think I was never before sad?" he asked. "It's okay. I like you should think about these things. I only wish I had a good answer. I don't know if there is one. I can only tell you what I know in here," he said, pounding his chest. "In my heart. And I know God was with me many times during the Holocaust. Times when I should have died. I have many stories...but they are not for little girls' ears." Mr. Goldblum shook his head and held his hands up as if to say he had told me all he thought I should hear.

But I wanted to hear more. I begged him not to stop and when he saw how much I wanted to listen, he finally gave in.

"Okay, okay...I tell you this story, my curious child," he gave in, straightening his *kippa* and running his hand through his beard. He took a deep breath, then began.

"In the camp, Treblinka, the German officers

liked to play games with the prisoners. We called them death games, because usually nobody returned alive. One night the officers forced some of us out of bed and into the yard in the center of the camp. Another death game was in store. I assumed this was my end. It was very cold and they didn't let us put on our coats or shoes. There was snow on the ground. They yelled at us to form a circle and entertain them with our dancing." Mr. Goldblum stopped for a moment and took another deep breath. He cleared his throat and spit some phlegm into his handkerchief. It was hard to believe what he was telling me had really happened.

"We took hold of each other and began to dance. There was a man named Yankel among us. He had a very beautiful voice. As we started to move, he began to sing quietly. We were starving and freezing and exhausted, but we huddled close together in our little circle and forced ourselves to dance. Yankel's singing grew louder. His voice pierced the cold night as if it were fire. I closed my eyes and suddenly my body began to feel warm all over. Around and around we went. Soon I felt as if I were drifting away with the joy of our dancing. We danced faster and faster. I opened my eyes. The other men also seemed joyful. It was the first time I had seen anyone smile in over a year. The louder Yankel sang, the faster we danced. I closed my eyes again and said out loud, '*Shema Yisrael Hashem Elokeinu Hashem Echad.*' Then I heard the man next to me say it, and the man next to him. Then bang!" Mr. Goldblum said loudly, clapping his hands. I jumped in my seat. I was picturing the whole thing so clearly in my mind.

"The first gunshot rang out," he continued. "I opened my eyes, thinking the end was finally here. I looked around for a dead body on the ground. There was none. I looked at the officer who had fired his gun. It was pointed to the sky. Into the air he had shot a bullet. He ordered us to stop. Yankel was quiet and we stopped dancing. We stood there waiting for more shots...but they never came. Instead, he ordered us back to our bunks. We all returned alive."

"But I don't get it. Why didn't he kill you?" I asked, still wondering what all this had to do with God.

"You must understand, Libby. Their greatest pleasure was to watch us suffer. There was nothing they wouldn't do. They loved to watch us beg for our lives, and sacrifice our integrity as Jews. To them it was a show. It made them laugh. But that night they couldn't break us. We had become joyful with our music. We were ready to die, proud to be Jewish, proud to believe in our one God. It would have given them no pleasure to kill us that night. Do you understand?"

I could understand why the officer had decided not to kill them that night. But I didn't see where God was. I shook my head, still confused.

"Ah, you don't see, do you?" Mr. Goldblum said. "In our dancing and Yankel's singing, God was. Deep in our souls and in our hearts when we said '*Shema Yisrael*'...you know what that means?"

I shook my head again.

" 'Hear, O Israel, the Lord is our God, the Lord is One.' It is a prayer the Jewish people have been reciting for three thousand years. It is what keeps us so strong. Even at the moment of our final suffering and execution, we repeated these words. We were ready to die, still believing in our one God. There was power in this. Can you see that? The power of God shows itself in many lights. That night it tricked evil and saved our lives. But it had to start in our own hearts first. We had to go on believing, in spite of our pain. You understand?"

Yes. I could understand that. For him. That night. But what about Katrina? Hadn't God been in her heart? I asked Mr. Goldblum.

He sighed deeply and looked away from me, wiping his forehead with his handkerchief. "I believe the Almighty was in her heart. But sometimes what we think is best isn't what God thinks is best. And what we see as bad is really good. Because it's for the best in the end, though we may not understand why until we enter *Olam Haba*. You know what that is? The world we enter after we die. There is no real death...only a parting from this world."

"You mean Heaven?" I asked.

Mr. Goldblum nodded.

"Libby! Libby!" Mandy ran over and wrapped herself around my legs. I lifted her up to my lap and gave her a big squeeze, glad to be holding her. My mind was whirling with so many new thoughts and ideas.

"I still don't know," I said, thinking aloud.

"You don't know what?" Mr. Goldblum asked.

"I just don't know what I believe."

"So think about it. In your heart you really do know," Mr. Goldblum said as he squeezed my hand.

*   *   *

I did think about it...all afternoon, in between swimming and practicing the piano and dinner. I thought about it so much I thought my brain would burst. Finally I curled up on the couch and turned on the television. Sometimes you just need to do that, to not think about anything at all.

Chapter 13

I had honestly planned to follow Mr. Goldblum's advice about speaking directly to Dad. But as the days passed, I could never seem to catch him at a good time. So when Rebecca called to invite me to a Jewish art fair, I miserably told her everything that had happened and said I doubted my parents would let me go.

"Oh, Libby, that's terrible!" she cried. "What are we going to do?"

"I don't know," I said. "I'll just have to wait until I can talk to my father."

"But that could take forever.... The fair is going to be so much fun."

"I can imagine," I grumbled.

Rebecca was silent for a moment. "But your father just said you couldn't come to me on Friday night. He didn't say anything about the rest of the week."

"Yeah, but you know that's probably what he meant."

"Ask your mother. They don't always answer the same."

"That's true...okay, I'll ask her and call you back."

But Mom said "no," using my father as an excuse. We got into an argument about it and I told her it wasn't fair to judge a person she hadn't even met. To my surprise, she agreed with me and decided it was time to finally meet "this Rebecca girl," as they called her. She told me to invite her over.

I called Rebecca immediately and we made plans for her to come over the next day after my classes. I could hardly wait. I thought of everything we'd do. We'd go swimming, and I'd teach her to play something on the piano, and I'd have Quana make us her delicious tacos for lunch. Once my mom saw how normal and nice Rebecca was, this whole mess would be cleared up. Why didn't I think of this before?

*　　　*　　　*

"I'll get it," I yelled, running to the door to let Rebecca in the next day.

"Hi."

"Hi! Come in."

"Wow!" she said, looking all around. "You didn't tell me it was so big!"

"Tacos! Tacos!" Mandy came running down the hall screaming. My mother followed. I introduced her to Rebecca.

"Hello, Rebecca," my mother said.

"Nice to meet you, Mrs. Ross," Rebecca replied. She always knew the polite thing to say.

"You're just in time for lunch. Come on, let's go into the kitchen," Mom said.

"Tacos!" Mandy called out as we all followed my mother into the kitchen.

"Libby," Rebecca whispered.

"What?"

"I brought my own lunch."

"So you'll stick it in the fridge," I said.

"Shh," she whispered again.

"Sorry," I said, lowering my voice to a whisper. "But why are we whispering?"

"I didn't want to make a scene in front of your mother."

"What scene? What are you talking about?" But before Rebecca could explain, we had reached the kitchen.

"I hope you like tacos, Rebecca," my mother said. "They're Libby's favorite."

Quana was putting all the stuff on the table: meat, lettuce, tomatoes, cheese, guacamole, taco sauce, and tortillas.

Rebecca looked at me with the strangest expression on her face. She didn't answer my mother.

"This is Quana," I finally said, breaking the silence. "She makes the world's greatest tacos."

Quana and Rebecca exchanged hellos.

"Tacos!" Mandy cried again.

"Hi, everyone," Sheila said, suddenly appearing in the kitchen. As usual, she was all decked out in too much makeup and some new outfit she'd conned my parents into letting her buy. I hadn't expected this to be such a family get-together. She usually ate at a friend's house. "Mm, tacos! What's the occasion?"

"Libby's new friend is here," Mom explained. "This is Rebecca."

"I'm starving," Sheila announced, plopping down in her seat and digging into the food on the table.

"Sheila, where're your manners?" my mom scolded. "Introduce yourself."

"Oh yeah...I'm Sheila," she said, crunching down noisily on a tortilla.

"Come on, girls, aren't you hungry?" my mother asked, putting a taco on each of our plates. "Dig in."

I started to fill my taco shell, but Rebecca just sat there.

"Don't be rude, Libby. Let Rebecca go first," Sheila said with a fresh smirk on her face.

"You're one to talk," I said, wishing I could tell her to shut up, which I would have if Rebecca hadn't been there.

"That's okay...I um...I can't eat it," Rebecca said.

"Why not? Are you a vegetarian or something?" Sheila asked.

"Or something," Rebecca said. Her face was getting all red.

"Food allergies?" Sheila continued.

"Not exactly," Rebecca hesitated.

"So what is it?" Sheila persisted.

"Sheila, please!" my mother warned.

But we were all staring at Rebecca, dying of curiosity.

Finally she told us. "I keep kosher," she said quietly.

"Oh dear, I'm sorry," my mother said. "Libby, why didn't you tell me?"

"What's 'kosher'?" I asked with a sinking feeling in my stomach. I had wanted to show my mother that Rebecca was really a normal kid. I had wanted to play down the Jewish stuff. Now she was popping another new idea on me. It was probably another *mitzvah*. Maybe this hadn't been such a good idea after all.

"It means she can't eat bacon and shrimp, for one thing," Sheila offered.

"How would you know?" I asked.

"I wasn't born yesterday."

"Girls, please. Rebecca, is there anything you can eat? I'm sure you're hungry," my mom said, going to the refrigerator.

"She brought her own lunch," I jumped in.

"Well why didn't you say so?" my mother said.

"That's okay, I'm not really hungry," Rebecca replied, still with a strange expression on her face.

"Nonsense. We don't want to eat in front of you. Eat your lunch," Mom urged.

Rebecca looked at me and slowly took a sandwich from her backpack. Then she whispered to me, "I didn't think there was going to be an audience. Excuse me for a minute," she said, getting up and going to the sink. Oh no, she was going to wash, just like we did over the *challah* on Shabbat! Why did I have to open my big mouth? Now I knew what Rebecca had meant when she'd said she didn't want to make a scene.

"Mrs. Gilbert gave me a new piano piece," I

said, trying to divert everyone's attention.

"What's she doing?" Sheila asked, ignoring me.

Rebecca took a coffee cup and poured water over her hands, then dried them and murmured a blessing.

"Washing," I said as Rebecca returned to the table, quickly mumbled *Hamotzi*, and took a bite of her sandwich. "And blessing her food."

My mother looked on silently.

"To each his own," Sheila shrugged, breaking the silence. "So what else can't you eat?"

"Sheila, don't put Rebecca on the spot." My mother shot Sheila a warning glance. "Libby tells me you have a brother and two sisters," she said politely to Rebecca.

"Yes, and one on the way."

"I don't know how your mother does it," Mom marvelled, wiping Mandy's face.

"Yeah, she can barely manage with three," Sheila said about my mother as she noisily stuffed another taco into her mouth.

My mom looked disapprovingly at Sheila but didn't say anything.

"Well it's not exactly easy being a mother," Rebecca pointed out, "no matter how many children you have. But she has me and my sister Sarah to help."

My mother smiled approvingly at Rebecca.

"Don't you have a maid?" Sheila asked.

"Not everyone has a maid," my mother said, sounding more and more irritated with Sheila. Next to her, Rebecca was beginning to look like an angel. Good.

"Hello, everybody," Abby shouted, coming into the kitchen. For once I was happy to see her. It would take the attention away from Rebecca.

"Very interesting lunch with the producers. You won't believe what went on," Abby said to my mother.

"Something good, I hope," my mom said.

"In the end, yes, thanks to me. You ready to work?"

"In a minute. We're just finishing up. This is Libby's friend, Rebecca. Remember the one I was telling you about?" my mother reminded her. I wondered just what she had told Abby.

Abby suddenly seemed interested, or curious, or nosey. "Oh...how do you do, honey?" she said.

"Hi," Rebecca answered quietly.

"Sheila, will you please wipe Mandy's tray and clean her up?" Mom asked Sheila.

"What do we pay Quana for?" Sheila retorted.

"I don't like your attitude at all today, young lady!" my mother snapped. "Just do as I say." Sheila rolled her eyes and stuck her tongue out at my mother when she wasn't looking, then did as she was told.

Abby sat down and started to nibble on some lettuce and ask Rebecca questions about herself. It was the strangest gathering of people I'd ever seen at one table: Abby, Miss Hip Hollywood; Sheila, Miss Teenage Terror; Rebecca, Miss Orthodox Jew; and me, Miss Fool. What had I gotten myself into?

After a few minutes of Rebecca answering different questions, my mother got up from the table. "I think Rebecca's had enough," she said. "Libby, you can go to the art fair on Thursday. Come on, Abby, we have a lot of work to do." She rose to leave the room and Abby followed.

I looked at Rebecca and we both started to laugh. I just knew Mom would like her once she got to know her. Mandy started to laugh along with us.

"What's so funny?" Sheila demanded.

"For once you said all the right things," I said to Sheila.

"What are you talking about?"

If she'd only known.

Chapter 14

REBECCA was right. The art fair was a lot of fun. There were all kinds of neat things to look at and buy: sculptures, tapestries, stained glass, jewelry, dolls, toys, clothes. And everything was handmade by artists.

It was a hot day, so after walking around for a while we bought Cokes and sat down in a shady spot under a tree.

"I guess Coke is kosher," I said.

"It sure is."

"What makes something kosher anyway?" I asked, still curious about this whole business.

Rebecca explained that kosher meat was different from regular meat. It had to be bought from a special butcher to make sure it met certain standards. But that wasn't all there was to it. They weren't allowed to blend milk products with meat, either.

"Like putting cheese in your tacos?" I asked.

"Right."

"Next you'll be telling me you can't drink a milkshake with a hamburger," I joked.

"I can't," Rebecca said. "It's not just mixing them. We can't even eat them together at the same meal. And we have to wait six hours after eating meat before we can eat dairy foods again."

"So you've never had a cheeseburger?"

"Right."

"Boy, you don't know what you're missing."

"Are they that good?"

I nodded, feeling a little guilty. Why should I tempt Rebecca with what she could never have? Then again, I wondered, did she ever wish she could just eat whatever she wanted? I decided to ask.

"Do you ever wish you weren't *frum*?"

Rebecca was thoughtful for a moment. "Well...sometimes I wish..." she hesitated to go on. "Not that I weren't *frum*. But sometimes I wonder what it would be like not to be."

"Could you ever decide not to be?" I asked.

"Oh no...I could never. I mean...I could, but I wouldn't."

"Why not?"

"I don't really know," Rebecca admitted, chewing on her lower lip. "I've just always been this way. This is who I am."

I didn't think that was a very good answer. It was important to think about things. It was important to know why you did what you did. Otherwise you were nothing more than a robot. I told Rebecca what I was thinking. At first she was a little offended, but after discussing it for a while she understood what I meant.

"I'm not a robot. I mean, if I think about it, I can find the reasons for everything I do. It's just that nobody's ever questioned me before. All my friends are—"

"*Frum* like you," I finished for her.

"Yeah. Anyway, I really do like being this way. I mean, I was born Jewish. This is how God wants Jewish people to live. I think God knows best, don't you?"

I couldn't answer that. I still had too many doubts, too many questions about everything. "Do you really believe in God? I mean really?" I asked.

Rebecca nodded firmly. "Don't you?"

"Sometimes I think I really do. Like when I'm lighting candles on Shabbat. I get this feeling deep inside of me that's hard to describe. And I think maybe that's God. Or when I see something really beautiful, like a rainbow or a rose. Then I think there has to be a God. But when bad things happen, like what happened to Mr. Goldblum and the Jews in the Holocaust...well, then I start having my doubts."

"What happened to Mr. Goldblum?" Rebecca asked.

I forgot I hadn't shared all that with her. Or with anyone, for that matter. I'd been keeping it all to myself. I told Rebecca all about Katrina and Mr. Goldblum and Auschwitz. It felt good to finally be talking all this out with someone. You have to do that or you can drive yourself crazy.

When I finished telling Rebecca everything, we both sat in silence for a few moments, each deep in our own thoughts. It felt like the fair was a million miles away.

"Here's what I think," Rebecca finally said. "Well, not so much what I think, but what I've been taught. What the Torah teaches us, I mean. And I believe the Torah is true." She paused to gather her thoughts. "A person's got to...you just have to believe that God really is good and really is wise. I mean, He has to be to have masterminded all of Creation, right? And you have to believe that He created us because He loves us. So everything that happens must be for the best. Even if we can't understand it all the time. Even if it seems bad...it really is good...in the end."

"Sounds like what Mr. Goldblum says."

"It's what the Torah says."

"But how could the Holocaust have been for the best?"

Rebecca took one last, long gulp of her Coke and crumpled up the empty cup. "I don't know. But my father once said that if we use the Holocaust as an excuse not to believe in God, then it's as if Hitler really won the war. Do you know what I mean?"

"Not really," I said, shaking my head.

Rebecca continued to explain. "That's just what Hitler wanted: For us to forget the whole thing. To not believe in God anymore. To not be Jewish anymore. See what I mean?"

I thought about this for a minute. I could see

what she meant. "You make it all seem so easy. So simple to just believe."

"For me it's harder to believe that there isn't a God. Without God you can't explain anything at all."

"Yeah, I guess that's true. But—"

"But nothing. Sometimes you think too much, Libby. Come on, let's go look at some more booths. I want to see if I can find my mom a birthday present." Rebecca jumped up and brushed herself off.

Maybe I did think too much, and that was why I never felt satisfied. But if you didn't think, how would you ever find the truth?

"Libby, come on," Rebecca called again. I followed her towards some new booths, leaving my thoughts for another time.

"Oh, Rebecca, look!" I cried the minute I saw it. "It's perfect for Mr. Goldblum." I was looking at a watercolor painting of an old man sitting in a chair, reading a book to a young girl. It could have been Mr. Goldblum and I or it could have been he and Katrina. It could be whatever he wanted it to be. "I have to buy it for him."

"But can you?" Rebecca asked, gawking at the price tag.

The painting was eighteen dollars. I looked in my wallet. My mother had given me five dollars and I still had five left from what I'd taken from Abby. I was eight dollars short. "I guess not," I said. But that wasn't what I was thinking. I knew of a sure way to come up with the money. The fair would still be on tomorrow so I could come back and buy the painting. I didn't mention anything to Rebecca. Somehow I knew she wouldn't have approved of my plans.

*   *   *

The next morning I waited for Mom and Abby to get busy in the study. Then I headed for the kitchen. I knew what I had to do. Good...there it was in its usual place. I tiptoed over to Abby's purse and pulled out her wallet. Even though I'd done this two times already, I was still nervous. My heart was beating really fast and my hands were shaking. As always Abby had gobs of cash. Quickly I pulled out eight dollars and stuffed it into my pocket. Ah, safe! Or so I thought....

"Oh hello, honey!" It was Abby! I quickly threw the wallet into her purse and turned around. I could feel my face get all hot and red.

"I just needed to get something from my purse," she said, looking around for it. "Did I leave it in here?"

"Um...I don't know," I said, feeling weak in the knees.

"Wasn't it on the table?" Abby started to move towards me.

I didn't answer. I moved aside, revealing her purse. Oh, please don't notice anything, I thought. I turned and watched her reach into her purse. Oh no. I could see that when I'd thrown the wallet back, it had opened up and a bunch of cash had fallen out. I was doomed.

Abby turned around and looked at me with a surprised expression on her face. "Libby, were you taking money from—"

But before she could finish I dashed out the back door, hopped on my bike, and rode as fast as I could down the street. My heart was beating so fast I thought I would die. I could never go back home now and face Abby and my mom. I could only think of one safe place to go....

I turned the corner and headed for the Golden Years Retirement Home.

Chapter 15

I found Mr. Goldblum standing by the window, wrapped in his *tallit*. He was holding his prayer-book and swaying back and forth, like I'd seen the men do in shul. I figured he was praying, or *davening* as they called it. I waited quietly by the door for him to finish. "Hi," I finally said when he closed his book.

He was surprised to see me. "Libby! Come in, *maidelah*. What wind blows you here in the *mitten derinen*?"

"Mittender what?"

Mr. Goldblum laughed. "In the middle of everything. Come, come closer. Let me get a look at you."

As I walked over to Mr. Goldblum I could feel that stupid old lump in my throat getting bigger. He sensed something was wrong right away.

"Such a long face. Come, sit down with me. Tell me what's wrong."

I swallowed hard to fight back tears. "She's so rich, what does it matter? And she's such a phoney. I hate her," I managed to say, but then I couldn't talk anymore.

"Shh, *maidelah*. Shh. Come here," Mr. Goldblum held out his arms. I walked over and let him hug me. He patted my back and shushed me quietly. His *tallit* was still draped over his shoulders and for some reason it made him seem so much bigger and taller than he really was. I couldn't remember the last time my dad had held me like that. I felt so safe in his arms. Finally I began to calm down.

"There, now tell me what happened."

Mr. Goldblum listened quietly as I explained it all to him, from beginning to end. I told him how first I'd taken the money because my mom was too busy to give me any. Then I'd taken some for poor Berthenia. And finally because I wanted to buy the painting for him. I told him about how rich Abby was and how she acted like she liked us, but really she thought we were pests and wanted us out of her hair so she and my mother could write their stupid screenplay.

I felt so relieved to tell Mr. Goldblum everything. I knew he would understand. But when I finally finished and took notice of the serious expression on his face, I began to think I'd made a mistake. Mr. Goldblum was looking at me without smiling. Suddenly I started to think that maybe he was just like every other adult. Maybe he didn't understand me at all.

"Are you mad at me, too, Mr. Goldblum?" I asked.

"Mad? No, *maidelah*, I'm not mad. Disappointed, yes. Mad, no."

Hearing him say that made me want to cry all over again. I swallowed hard. "But all she ever spends her money on is getting her nails done and buying expensive jogging suits. She doesn't care about people like you and Berthenia. She's a big, selfish phoney who only cares about herself!"

"So you think she deserves to have her money taken away?" Mr. Goldblum asked.

I didn't answer. I needed to think about it.

"Go splash your face and have some water. Then come back and we'll talk about it," Mr. Goldblum said.

I went to the bathroom and looked at myself in the mirror. My face was all smudged from crying and my eyes were red. I looked ugly and I didn't like myself very much at that moment.

"Libby, did you fall in the toilet?" Mr. Goldblum called in to me.

"No," I said, watching a small smile creep over my face.

"Come, let's talk." I went back out to Mr. Goldblum. "That's much better, no?"

"Yes," I admitted, walking over to the picture of Katrina. "I wish I were as pretty as she was."

"Yes, she was a beautiful child. But so are you."

"Don't lie."

"I never lie."

"Well I don't feel so pretty today," I said.

"Perhaps it is because you don't feel right. When we are unhappy on the inside, we don't feel so good on the outside."

"I'm not sure how I feel." I sat down and looked around the room. My gaze fell on the ugly painting on his wall. "But it was such a nice painting. You would have loved it," I promised.

Mr. Goldblum got up slowly and walked over to his night table. He picked up a book and sat down next to me with it. It was the Bible. He flipped through the pages and found what he was looking for. He showed me the Ten Commandments. "Thou shalt not steal" was the eighth one.

"But this is different," I protested. "Abby doesn't need the money. And she's so selfish."

"Hitler also justified his actions," Mr. Goldblum said.

"What do you mean?" I demanded. I was beginning to feel really fidgety. I was beginning to wish I hadn't come here at all.

Mr. Goldblum explained, "The Nazis robbed from the Jews. Everything they took. They broke into our homes and helped themselves to our hard-earned possessions. As if they had every right."

"But we didn't deserve it," I said.

"Ah. But they thought we did. They believed we were greedy and selfish. They became our judges and decided they were more worthy of our things than we were."

"But Abby really and truly is greedy!" I continued to argue.

"Do you really know that?" Mr. Goldblum asked.

"Yes!" I said, getting more and more excited.

"Just like Hitler knew that every Jew was greedy?"

"But he couldn't have known that!" I declared, standing up. Mr. Goldblum pulled me back down and held my hands but I jerked them away. It wasn't the same thing!

"Libby...listen to me. Do you really know how Abby spends her money? Perhaps she gives a lot to charity."

"I doubt it!"

"And do you really know Abby? Hate is a very strong word. Perhaps there are things you would like about her if you knew her better."

"I don't want to know her better."

"Then it isn't fair to be her judge."

I plopped down on the bed again without saying anything. I thought of the Nazis raiding people's homes, taking everything. It could have happened to me.

"But we weren't greedy. Hitler only thought we were," I persisted.

"Maybe some of us were," Mr. Goldblum said.

"Well that still didn't make it right," I blurted out before I realized what I was saying.

"Ha!" Mr. Goldblum cried, jumping up and clapping his hands. "You said it, not me!"

I thought of what I'd said. Even if we were greedy, it wasn't right for them to take what belonged to us. I could see that I'd done the same thing to Abby. Just because I didn't like her wasn't a reason to steal from her. If everybody did that, the whole world would be a bunch of thieves.

Mr. Goldblum came over to me and put his hands on my shoulders. "You must go home and face them, Libby. Perhaps you will reach an understanding."

I didn't move or say anything. I didn't want to go. I was afraid.

"You must go," Mr. Goldblum repeated, giving me a little push towards the door.

"If you really cared, you wouldn't make me leave," I said, feeling like I was going to cry all over again.

"It's because I care that I make you go. You will see. Everything will be all right."

"How can you know that?" I asked as I reached the door.

"I never lie."

I rode my bike home slowly. I wasn't in any rush at all.

Chapter 16

ON my way home, I carefully thought out what I would say to Abby and my mother. Hopefully by the time my dad got home the whole mess would be cleared up and he wouldn't have to get involved. It was a good thing I didn't know I had another thing coming, or I wouldn't have gone back home at all.

Just as I was rounding the corner of our street, I heard a car honking its horn. I moved onto the sidewalk, but the honking didn't stop so I turned to look. Oh no, it was Mom! Her station wagon pulled up alongside of me. She was already yelling at me, even though I couldn't hear a word she was saying through the closed window. I got off my bike but kept walking. My mom rolled down her window and leaned over.

"I've been looking for you everywhere!" she thundered. "Where in God's name have you been?"

I didn't answer. I just kept walking. Suddenly I

didn't feel at all like apologizing.

"Stop this minute!" she screamed.

I finally stopped, but I couldn't bring myself to look her in the eyes. A car pulled up behind us and honked impatiently. My mother waved for them to go around. She looked at me and shook her head back and forth in disbelief. Then she told me to get my "you know what" back on my bike and back to the house immediately, where she'd be waiting for me.

When I got home Mom was waiting in the hall by the front door. I could see Abby sitting on the couch in the den, listening. "What could have possibly gotten into you?" my mother demanded.

Now what did she think I could say to that? I knew I should say I was sorry, but I didn't feel like it anymore. She shook her head and threw up her hands. "You exasperate me, Libby. Go to your room until your father gets home."

"But—"

"Save your 'buts' for later. I only want to deal with this once. I just don't have the energy—"

"Or the time," I interrupted. You would think this would have been more important than her writing.

"Don't be fresh with me!"

"I'd rather be fresh than stale!" I blurted out. I don't know what had come over me. I was only making her angrier. But I just couldn't stop myself.

"To your room! Now!" my mother ordered as the phone rang.

On the way to my room I heard Abby ask my

mother if she had to be so hard on me. I couldn't believe it. Maybe Mr. Goldblum was right. Maybe there was a side to Abby I didn't know. Maybe.

*　　　*　　　*

Wouldn't you know, my dad still wasn't home by eight o'clock. Quana finally brought some food up to me but I wasn't very hungry. An hour or so later Sheila popped her head in.

"Boy, are you going to get it when Dad gets home," she said.

"Thanks for the big news bulletin," I retorted.

"You're welcome," Sheila smirked. "Mom's mad at Dad because he didn't call to say he'd be late."

"Typical," I said.

"Poor Mom. First you and then Dad."

"You're one to talk."

"What do you mean?"

"I know what you and your friends are up to."

"Oh sure you do. Don't make me laugh."

"I heard you sneaking Mom's car out last Friday night."

"You little spy! Why don't you mind your own business?"

"What's going on in there?" my mom called up when she heard us arguing. "Sheila, don't you have homework?"

"I'm all finished," Sheila called back in her sweetest voice.

"Well then, find something else to do. Libby's being punished."

"I'll practice my cheers," she said, sticking her butt out at me as she walked away.

I stuck my tongue out at her and slammed my door. Then I put on my pajamas and got into bed. But I was too upset to sleep. What a sister...what a mother...what a father...what a family! Why couldn't we be like Rebecca's family? Why couldn't we all get along with each other and spend time together and not fight all the time, and just love each other? That's what a family was supposed to do, wasn't it?

I don't remember what time it was when I finally fell asleep, but I could hear my mom's computer in the study and my dad still hadn't come home.

*   *   *

The next morning my dad was already gone by the time I woke up. Mom grounded me in my room until he got home that night. I could have gone into *The Guinness Book of World Records* for the kid who had to wait the longest to be punished.

It seemed like the day was going to drag on forever. But finally Dad got home. I listened to him fix himself a drink and say hello to Mandy. By now I just wanted to get the whole thing over with. I was sick of waiting. Finally he came to my room.

"Where's your mother?" he asked as he sat down at my desk.

"She had to run over to Abby's for something."

"I told her I'd be home at five," he said. I could tell he was annoyed. Then again, he was hardly one to talk about being home on time.

"Well," my father began, "what's the story?"

Story? If it was a story he wanted, why didn't he go to my mother? She was the writer.

"Didn't Mom tell you?"

"Yes, but I want you to tell me."

"If you already know, I don't see why I have to tell you." Why did he have to make this so hard for me? I felt bad enough as it was.

"I'm waiting," he said, getting more and more irritated.

"Mom's always busy writing, and you're never around," I started.

"Don't change the subject, young lady."

All the rest of the time I'm just a kid who's too young to understand. But suddenly when my parents are mad at me I'm a young lady. I wish they'd make up their minds.

"But it *is* the subject," I insisted.

"The subject is you, Libby," my dad continued. "I understand you took money from Abby. I'd like you to explain."

"She wouldn't let me play the piano. She called Bach 'noise,' " I continued to protest, but I could see it wasn't doing any good.

"That's a reason? I just don't understand," he sighed, taking a long sip of his drink and swishing the ice around.

Okay, so it wasn't a good reason. I knew that now. No reason was a reason to steal. If only my dad would have let me explain why I had done it in the first place, even if I knew it was wrong now.

But he wasn't listening; I mean, really listening. He never did. And I was having a hard time putting it into words. Yes, I didn't like Abby. But it was much more than that. It was my mother. And him, too. They were the real reason why. I searched for the words, but couldn't find them. I got up and went over to look out my window. The candlesticks were still resting on my ledge. I remembered it was Friday. What a way to spend Shabbat.

"This is very serious, Libby," my father said.

"I'm sorry," I finally mumbled. I didn't know what else to say.

"Sorry isn't enough."

"So I'll save up my allowance and pay her back!" I offered, feeling myself get all worked up. It wasn't fair. I was trying to apologize.

My father took another sip of his drink and looked at me long and hard. I couldn't stand it and looked away. I just stood there fidgeting with the candlesticks. Mr. Goldblum hadn't told me what to do if saying sorry wasn't enough.

"Hi, Dad!" Sheila said, strolling into the room. She was dressed in her new cheerleader outfit. She was all sweetness and smiles and boy, did my dad fall for it.

"Hi, Sheila. Good, I'm glad you're home. I think this is a family matter."

Sheila planted a big kiss on my dad's cheek, then sat down on the bed next to him. He smiled at her. "How was practice?" he asked.

"Great. We learned two new cheers."

"Don't they have cheerleaders at Libby's school? I think she needs to be involved in something to keep her out of trouble."

"She's only in sixth grade, Dad. Next year she can try out."

"I'm not going to be a stupid cheerleader," I said.

"It isn't stupid," Sheila replied.

"Please, girls. Sheila, what do you think about all of this?" my dad asked her.

I couldn't believe he was asking her, of all people! If he'd only known what she'd been up to.

"Well, I think you're right. She should be involved in something to keep her out of trouble."

That was it. I couldn't stand it anymore. She was such a faker! My anger got the best of me, and I finally let the cat out of the bag, though I knew I'd regret it:

"Ha! Being a cheerleader hasn't kept you out of trouble! You and your friends think you're so cool, sneaking the car out at night and cruising around town!"

Sheila's face turned bright red with anger. If she'd been a dog she would have bit me for sure. "Liar!" she yelled.

"I am not!"

My father looked from me to Sheila and back at me again.

"Libby, why would you say something like that?" Of course he believed Sheila and not me, but I wasn't going to give up.

"I may be a thief, but I'm not a liar. You're

never around to see what's really going on."

"What's going on in here?" my mother demanded, coming into my room.

"I wish I knew," my dad said angrily as he stood up. "If you'd been home on time you'd have heard the whole thing."

"You have got a lot of nerve, Irving. Sometimes I really can't believe you!"

"It seems you have one daughter who's a thief and another who's a delinquent!" my dad continued.

"Not me, Irv. We. They're *our* daughters!"

"I am not a delinquent!" Sheila yelled and ran from the room.

"Not so fast, little girl," Dad hollered, going after her. Why was she a little girl when he was mad but I was a young lady?

My mom looked at me. I was still standing in front of the candlesticks. "Good Shabbos," I said sarcastically.

"Don't be fresh, Libby."

I bit my tongue so as not to say anything. I could hear my dad and Sheila begin to argue.

"We'll deal with this later," my mother said as she followed my father to Sheila's room.

I stood by my door and listened. Pretty soon Mom was blaming Dad and Dad was blaming Mom. Sheila was crying in the background as they yelled at each other. I covered my ears with my hands as their voices rose. Finally I couldn't stand it anymore. I slammed my door and threw myself down on my bed. I hated it here! If only...if only...yes...that was it....

I opened my door quietly and stood in the hallway, listening. I could hear Sheila sobbing in her room and Mom and Dad arguing in their bedroom. There was so much noise, nobody even heard me open the front door and leave the house. It was growing darker by the minute, so I ran as fast as I could to Rebecca's house.

Chapter 17

BY the time I got to Rebecca's it was almost sundown. Of course she was surprised to see me.

"Libby! What are you doing here?"

I was out of breath. "May I come in?" I panted.

"Rebecca, is the table set?" Mrs. Klein called from the kitchen.

"Yes, Ema!" she called back. The smell of dinner cooking filled the living room. The candles were all lined up, ready to be lit. Everything was just as it should be. It made me want to cry.

"But what about your parents? I thought—" Rebecca began.

"They don't know I'm here."

"What? I don't under—" she started, but I interrupted her again.

"It's a long story....I can stay, can't I?"

Rebecca bit her lower lip.

"Then help Chana get dressed," Mrs. Klein said, coming out of the kitchen. "Libby! I didn't know you were coming for Shabbos."

"I wasn't sure I could come until the last minute," I said, thinking fast. "I hope it's all right."

"Of course it is. Rebecca, set another place and then both of you can help Chana and Aaron get dressed and straighten the bedroom. I have to shower."

"Okay. Come on, Libby," Rebecca said, taking me by the hand and rushing me to her bedroom. As she dressed the kids and tidied up, I told her the whole story from beginning to end.

"Maybe we should tell my parents," she suggested. "They'll know what to do."

"Are you crazy? They'll only call my parents."

"Yeah, I guess you're right. But what about yours? Don't you think they'll come looking for you?"

"Knowing them, it will take a long time before they even notice I'm gone. And they probably won't think of you right away."

"But what if they come here?"

"Rebecca...Libby...we're waiting for you. It's time to light," Mrs. Klein called.

"Coming!" Rebecca shouted as we switched off her light and went to the living room.

After lighting, Rebecca and I played with Chana, Aaron, and Sarah in the living room while we waited for Mr. Klein to come home from shul. The room had that peaceful Shabbat glow I loved so much, and for a little while I forgot the real reason I was there.

Mr. Klein finally got home and we all went to the table to make *Kiddush*. Before Mr. Klein recited *Kiddush* we always sang a special song that welcomes in Shabbat. We were on the second verse when there was a knock at the door.

"Were you expecting anyone?" Mrs. Klein said to Mr. Klein as she rose to answer the door. Mr. Klein shook his head and kept on singing.

I got a sick feeling in my stomach and looked at Rebecca. She bit her lip as she watched her mother go to the door. I hadn't planned on them finding me so soon. I listened as Mrs. Klein opened the door and heard my father's voice. I couldn't make out what he was saying because Mr. Klein and the other kids were still singing.

Before I could say "bubble gum," Mrs. Klein was standing at the foot of the dining room table with my parents beside her. They were silent as they waited for Mr. Klein and the other kids to finish singing. There wasn't much I could do except sit there and pray with all my heart that my parents wouldn't embarrass me in front of everyone. They both looked like they might explode any minute. But I knew they wouldn't...they couldn't, not in front of the Kleins.

"Yitz, this is Irv and Doris Ross, Libby's parents," Mrs. Klein said once the singing stopped.

Mr. Klein rose and shook my father's hand. "It's a pleasure. Libby didn't tell us you were coming. Rebecca, set two more places."

"Yitz, I don't think the Kleins plan to stay for dinner," Mrs. Klein explained. Obviously my parents had filled her in.

"I don't understand," Mr. Klein said.

But before my parents could explain I jumped up from the table. "I'm not going home with you!" I cried out. I ran to Rebecca's room and locked the door behind me. I could hear chairs rustle and all kinds of commotion. Chana started to cry. Everyone seemed to be talking at once.

A few minutes later my dad was knocking at the door. "Libby, please open the door," he said, trying to stay calm.

I didn't answer.

"Libby, please. Open the door. I'm not going to yell through a wall." His voice was getting louder.

I still didn't say anything.

Then my mother came to the door. She was trying to sound calm. "Libby, please come out. We're not going to be mad at you. We just want to talk."

Sure. I didn't believe that for a minute. As soon as we'd get in the car they'd start yelling at me. They didn't want to listen to what I had to say. They were just trying to be nice in front of the Kleins.

"No!" I finally screamed. "I don't want to live with you anymore! I'm staying here with Rebecca!" It wasn't like I planned to say that or anything. I didn't even know that's how I felt. I just blurted it out without thinking about it. But once I'd heard my own words, I realized that really was how I felt. I really didn't want to live there anymore. Not unless things changed.

There was a long silence. Then I heard muffled voices but I couldn't make out what they were saying. I heard footsteps in the hall and then they were gone. I didn't know what to do next. I hadn't planned on making a big scene like this. It was as if a volcano had erupted inside of me and I couldn't help myself.

A few minutes later there was a knock on the door. "Libby, open up, it's me." It was Rebecca.

"Is it just you?"

"Yes, I promise."

I let her in. "Are your parents mad at me?" I asked.

"I don't know. But they're sure mad that I didn't tell them."

"I'm sorry."

"It's okay."

"What are they doing out there?"

"My parents are talking to yours."

"It won't do any good."

"Maybe it will."

"I wish we were sisters," I said.

Rebecca sat down on the bed next to me. "Me, too," she replied.

A few minutes later, Mrs. Klein knocked on the door and Rebecca let her in. I thought she'd be angry at me, too, but she wasn't. She came over and sat down next to Rebecca and me.

"It's very important to honor your mother and father," she said tenderly.

"But—" I started.

"Your parents are very worried about you," she interrupted.

Well they should be, I thought but didn't say. If only Mrs. Klein understood. I wondered what my parents had told her.

"We've invited them for dinner," Mrs. Klein continued. I looked at Rebecca. She was as surprised as I was. I couldn't believe this was happening.

Mrs. Klein asked us both to come back to the table, but I didn't think I could bear to face everyone. I told Rebecca to go without me. But Rebecca tried to convince me it was the best thing that could have happened.

"Don't you see, Libby? Now they'll have a chance to see why you love Shabbat so much."

I wasn't so sure about that. "Rebecca!" Mrs. Klein called from the dining room.

"Please come with me," Rebecca pleaded.

"I don't know."

"You can't stay in here forever."

"Why not?"

"You're not being sensible. Besides, you're safe as long as you're here. Your parents wouldn't dare make a scene in front of my parents."

"Okay," I finally said and followed Rebecca into the dining room to see what was in store for me.

Chapter 18

I sat back down at the table without looking at anybody. The whole situation was so uncomfortable...and it was all my fault. I could feel my parents watching me. Finally I looked at my mother. She smiled at me and I was surprised to see her eyes fill with tears. Had I upset her that much? I glanced at my dad. He didn't look like he was going to explode anymore. Instead he looked kind of sad. Like he did that night a few months ago in Connecticut when I was the only one left in the kitchen for him to tell about his promotion. I started to feel a little sorry for saying the things I'd said and embarrassing them like this.

Everyone stood up as Mr. Klein poured the wine and began to recite *Kiddush*. A hush filled the room as his deep, clear voice sang the Hebrew words. I glanced at my father. He had a faraway look in his eyes. What was he thinking? I kept watching him, and as Mr. Klein continued reciting

Kiddush something unbelievable happened. I was sure my father wasn't aware of it himself. But I was. I looked at Rebecca and so was she. We both saw it: my father's lips moving quietly along with Mr. Klein, reciting the Hebrew words to himself under his breath. He knew the blessing! He knew it! I glanced at my mother. She was staring at my father, too, unaware that I was looking at her. She had tears in her eyes.

After *Kiddush* we went into the kitchen to wash, as usual. Mrs. Klein showed my mother how to do the ritual washing and say the Hebrew blessing. But my father told her he knew what to do. I looked at him with wonderment as he quickly washed and quietly said the blessing. He knew I was staring at him, but he didn't look at me. What was going on?

When we got back to the table to say *Hamotzi* over the *challah*, Mr. Klein motioned to my father to see if he'd like to have the honor. My father looked around the table at everyone and hesitated. Then quickly, he reached for the two loaves of bread and the knife. Rebecca and I looked at each other in amazement as my father lifted the loaves and took a deep breath. Then he said the blessing softly and slowly. I felt a lump rising in my throat. I didn't think my father knew anything about being Jewish. Where had he learned all of this? And why had he kept it a secret all these years? I watched as my father sliced the bread and passed it around to everyone. For once I was too baffled to think.

Nobody said anything for a few moments and there was a long and awkward silence. Rebecca kicked me under the table and I kicked her back.

"This is delicious," my mother finally said. "Did you bake it?"

"Not this week. Lately it seems there just aren't enough hours in the day," Mrs. Klein sighed. "It's from Moshe's bakery. It is good, isn't it?" she said, rising to go to the kitchen.

"I could make a meal out of this alone," my mom declared.

"They eat it every week, for Shabbat," I said.

Neither my mother nor my father responded to me. I guess I was asking for trouble so I decided to just be quiet.

"Libby really enjoys spending Shabbat with you," my mother told Mr. Klein. I was glad she was being so polite, but I noticed my father didn't seem so thrilled about her comment. I sensed his mood changing again.

"Well she's the perfect guest. She always keeps me on my toes with all of her questions," Mr. Klein replied.

"I'm sure she does. Libby's always been our curious child," my mother continued. I could tell my father was getting more and more irritated. But he still didn't say anything.

"That's good, that's good. If you're not curious, you never learn," Mr. Klein said.

"Curiosity can lead to trouble," my father finally mumbled.

For a moment no one said anything. The Kleins just stared at Dad.

"So how do you like living in Los Angeles?"

Mrs. Klein asked, breaking the silence.

"Oh, we love it!" my mother said enthusiastically. My father didn't say anything. There was another silence.

"Rebecca, bring the fish in, please," Mrs. Klein said.

Rebecca jumped up and went into the kitchen. She brought out a platter of gefilte fish and passed it around as the Kleins and my parents made small talk about Los Angeles.

"Mm, this is delicious," my mother said, taking a bite of fish.

"Thank you. That I did make."

"Daddy, tell about the fish in the kitchen sink," Sarah requested. Boy, was I glad for her interruption. The strained conversation was becoming unbearable.

"Sink! Sink!" Chana mimicked and laughed.

"Yeah, Abba, tell us!" Aaron joined in.

"You'd think they'd get tired of the same old story," Mr. Klein said. But I could tell he was glad to have something else to talk about. He proceeded to explain how his mother used to buy a live fish for Shabbat and let it swim in the kitchen sink until she was ready to make gefilte fish out of it.

My father ate quietly and listened. When Mr. Klein finished, Aaron and Sarah laughed. I even spotted a little smile on my dad's face.

"Thank God for refrigerators," Mrs. Klein said. "Can you imagine?"

"I never wanted her to kill the fish either," my father murmured.

"Your mother made her own, too?" Mrs. Klein asked.

Dad nodded, then looked down at his plate and took another bite of fish. How come he'd never told us that? How come he never talked about when he was growing up, for that matter? I realized there was so much about him I didn't know. Rebecca got up to clear the fish plates and I got up to help her, still too puzzled to say anything.

When the main course was served and everyone was sitting down again, Sarah showed her father the list of questions about the weekly Torah portion that she had brought home from her day camp. I didn't know any of the answers. They discussed the questions as we ate. My mother kept complimenting everything—the food, the dishes, the flowers on the table. My father just ate quietly without saying anything, but I could tell he was listening.

Then Aaron wanted his chance, too. He ran to his room and came back with his latest piece of artwork. While Mr. Klein was admiring it, Aaron started to get a little wild, as he usually did. He climbed onto the back of his father's chair and began making monkey sounds. Mr. Klein tickled him and pulled him down into his lap. Then Sarah wanted to get into the picture. She crawled under the table and started taking off her dad's shoes. "It's the shoe monster!" Mr. Klein cried, going along with the game. Aaron joined Sarah under the table.

"Not me!" Rebecca shouted when Aaron attacked her feet. "Mom, make him stop!"

"Ah!" I started to laugh. Sarah had pulled off my left shoe and was tickling my foot. Rebecca was laughing, too. "Mom!" she cried.

"Yitz, tell them to stop already. It's enough," Mrs. Klein finally said. "It's the one time all week...he always lets them go a little crazy," she tried explaining to my parents.

Mr. Klein finally told them to stop and sit back down in their chairs, but it took a few more minutes before things quieted down. I got my shoes back on and looked at my parents. They were sitting politely, eating in silence, watching everything that was going on. I wondered what they were both thinking. How could they not see how nice it could be...eating together...Shabbat...being a family. I wondered what they would do with me when I got home. I would, after all, have to go home with them, unless I wanted to make another big scene. But I didn't think I wanted to do that. I was in enough trouble already for being a thief and now a runaway.

Mrs. Klein asked Rebecca to help clear the dishes. I jumped up to lend a hand. My mother looked at me with surprise every time I got up to help. I guess because we never lifted a finger at home. But that was because Quana did everything.

"Do you like to sing?" I heard Mr. Klein ask my father.

"Don't let me stop you," my father said. I guess that meant no.

Mr. Klein started to sing a song as we cleared the table. Aaron and Sarah joined in and Chana banged her spoon on her tray. We brought out dessert as Mr. Klein continued to sing. My father wasn't singing, but he followed along in the *bentcher*. And my mother was rocking back and forth a little, as if she was really enjoying the song. I noticed her eyes darting around the apartment, taking everything in. They finally settled on the candles burning across the way in the living room. She stared at them wistfully and didn't even seem to be aware that she was swaying with the music. Maybe Rebecca was right. It had been a good idea to invite them to stay.

"That's a nice tune," my mother said when Mr. Klein finished singing. "Does it have a name?"

"*Yom Shabbaton*," Mr. Klein answered. "It's one of my favorites."

"I never learned Hebrew. What do the words mean?" my mother asked. I was surprised that she was so interested.

Mr. Klein looked down at his *bentcher*. "Well, the beauty of the song gets somewhat lost in the translation, but it goes something like this. Shabbat is a day of rest that we are careful to honor. Israel has a covenant with God in which He told us to rest on Shabbat. We will keep our side of the agreement and look to God to keep His—to see that no harm befalls us."

My mother looked across the table at me and smiled. I wasn't sure what the smile meant, but I had a feeling it had something to do with her beginning to understand about Shabbat and why I liked coming here so much. I smiled back at her.

"And you who keep your side of the agreement, you don't feel fooled?" my father asked.

"I'm not sure what you mean," Mr. Klein responded.

"Irv, don't get started," my mother cautioned.

My father looked at her intently and took a deep breath. "Never mind," he said, appeasing my mother.

"No, please. Explain yourself. I don't mind," Mr. Klein urged, smiling at my mother.

My father looked at my mother again and this time she nodded her consent. My father continued, "I think it's rather obvious. I simply meant that you've kept your side of the agreement but God hasn't kept His. It's rather one-sided, wouldn't you say?"

"You think the Almighty hasn't kept His side?" Mr. Klein asked.

"With all due respect, just look around you. Only a blind man can't see all the harm that befalls us, to use your own words," my father said. It was hard to understand what he was getting at, but he seemed really disturbed. I hoped he wouldn't get upset all over again.

"One must have a clear understanding of harm on all its different levels before drawing any conclusions," Mr. Klein responded gently.

"I see only one way to understand it," my father snapped, sounding more and more irritated.

"Unfortunately, most people do. But the Torah teaches us that even pain and suffering come from God. And to that end they are good. We only have to learn to find the good."

"I don't think it's that simple," my father said.

"Who said anything about simple?" Mr. Klein

countered. He and my father looked at each other for a moment without saying anything.

"Abba, aren't you even going to eat your pie?" Aaron interrupted. Mr. Klein looked at him and smiled, then took a big bite of his pie.

"Mmmm, delicious," he said.

"I helped Ema make it!" Aaron shouted excitedly.

By now Chana and Sarah were running around making a lot of noise and it was getting pretty chaotic again. "I'd like to give this topic the attention it deserves. Why don't we *bentch* and adjourn to the other room, where it's quiet?" Mr. Klein suggested.

I still wasn't sure where this whole discussion was leading, but I was glad that my father and Mr. Klein were talking at all, even if they didn't agree. Maybe Mr. Klein could teach my father a thing or two. That is, if my father would listen.

But just then my father looked at his watch and stood up. "Perhaps another time," he said. He glanced over at my mother. She got the message and stood up, too.

"Thank you for your hospitality. Everything was delicious."

"But we didn't *bentch* yet!" Aaron called out. Mrs. Klein shushed him.

"Libby, are you ready?" my father asked.

Ready? For what? To get into their car and drive away from this warm, peaceful room with the candles burning, and Mr. Klein singing, and Aaron and Chana and Sarah running around happily, and the peach pie, and Rebecca and...no, I wasn't ready. But what could I do? I'd already embarrassed my parents enough. I couldn't make another scene. Then again, the thought of driving through traffic and getting home to Sheila blasting her rock 'n' roll and Quana watching T.V. ...it would ruin my whole Shabbat. I realized I now understood why we weren't supposed to do any of those things on Shabbat. I could see how they interfered with the whole mood and atmosphere. I knew I would have to go home, but I didn't have to let that prevent me from keeping Shabbat, right? Right! I knew what I had to do. I took a deep breath. "I'll come home," I began. "But you're not supposed to drive on Shabbat. I'd like to walk, please."

My father looked at my mother and back at me. "Don't be ridiculous, Libby. It's late."

"But it's still light," I said, glancing out the window. "And I know my way. It only takes fifteen minutes."

"I can walk her halfway!" Rebecca jumped in. "It's okay, isn't it?" She looked at her father for approval. Mr. Klein nodded.

"Please," I said softly. "It's important to me."

My mother sighed and looked at my father. "I think it's okay, Irv."

Everyone was looking at Dad. He looked at Mr. Klein and I could see some unspoken exchange take place between them. "Very well," he finally said. "Have it your way."

Mr. Klein extended his hand to my father. "Good Shabbos," he said. My father shook his hand.

"Goodnight," he said and was off.

Chapter 19

WHEN I got home my father was already in his study, his opera music blaring from behind the closed door. I wasn't sure what that meant, except that he wanted to be alone. I found my mother in the kitchen fixing herself some tea.

"I guess you're pretty mad at me," I said quietly. My mother turned around and looked at me. She blew on her tea, then took a sip.

"I don't really know what we are," she replied. Her voice was calm now.

"Aren't you going to punish me?" I asked.

"I think we'll talk about it in the morning. After Dad and I have had a chance to discuss it."

"Okay," I mumbled, turning to leave.

"Libby," my mother said.

I turned to look at her.

"They're a nice family, the Kleins."

"They are?" I said, surprised by her remark. "I mean, I know," I agreed.

"And all this Shabbat business...I think it's kind of nice."

"Really?" I said, feeling my heart start to pound faster in my chest.

"I want to say something else," my mother continued.

She hesitated, took a deep breath, and then began: "My writing is very important to me. I think you must know that."

"Yeah," I said, looking down at my feet.

"And I could never give it up."

"But—" I started to protest.

"Wait, let me finish," she interrupted. I stopped myself and we both stared at each other without saying anything. She took another deep breath, as if carefully planning her words. "I'm going to try to be a better mother," she finally said. "To you and Sheila and Mandy. You deserve more from me."

I didn't know what to say. I could feel a lump rising in my throat. My mother came over and ran her fingers through my hair, then kissed my forehead.

"Goodnight," she said softly and left me alone in the kitchen.

"Goodnight," I answered, feeling a warm and tingly sensation run up and down my whole body. I stood there for a few moments, smiling to myself. Then I poured myself a glass of milk and grabbed a cookie. On my way out I remembered I'd just eaten meat for dinner, so I exchanged the milk for a glass of juice.

I walked slowly to my room and replayed the whole evening over in my head as I changed into my pajamas. I headed for the bathroom to brush my teeth, still in a daze from everything that had happened. The door was locked and I could hear Sheila blow-drying her hair. I knew she'd be real mad at me. She'd probably tell all her friends and they'd give me the silent treatment. But what did I care? I didn't even like her friends. The truth is, I did care. Not about her friends but about Sheila. I didn't like us not getting along. We used to be friends. I knocked on the door.

"Who is it and what do you want?"

"It's me," I said.

"I'm busy."

"I need to brush my teeth."

"Well you'll just have to wait."

I sat down outside the door and waited. I heard her start to practice cheers while she blew her hair dry. I could tell she was purposely taking a long time. "Sheila, come on!" I yelled.

"Patience is a virtue," she yelled back.

"I'm going to go in my pants!" I started banging on the door and she opened it so fast that I fell in.

"Fink," she said as she left.

"Clean up your mess!" I demanded, looking at the pile of stuff she had left all over the counter. Of course she ignored me. I always had to clean up after her.

I brushed my teeth and looked at myself in the mirror. I don't know why it was always so interesting to look at myself. I mean, I'd seen myself a billion times. But every time I looked it seemed like I'd see something just a little different. Like I could never quite get used to myself. I tried to imagine how I'd look after I'd had braces and my teeth were straight. It seemed like that time would never come. Why is it that the future takes so long to get here, but when you look back it seems like everything goes so fast? Then I realized one day I'd be looking back on all of this. I wondered how it would all turn out. If only I could look into a crystal ball and see the future.

I went back to my room and climbed into bed. But I kept tossing and turning and couldn't fall asleep. I finally decided to get another glass of juice. As I approached the kitchen, I was surprised to see the light on. I tiptoed closer and quietly peeked through the door. I saw my father sitting at the kitchen table. That was strange. He was looking at something on the table in front of him. A big book or something. He turned a page, then stopped, took out a handkerchief, and wiped his eyes. Could he be crying? One part of me figured he probably didn't want to be disturbed. But the curious part of me won, as usual, and I entered the kitchen.

"Dad?" I said quietly.

I startled him and he jumped.

"Libby...what are you doing up?" When he turned around I could see that his eyes were red.

"I couldn't sleep. I was thirsty," I replied, walking to the refrigerator. "You want something?" I asked, pouring myself a glass of orange juice.

"No thank you."

I'd been waiting so long to be alone with my father. Now that I finally was, one part of me felt shy and uncomfortable and wanted to leave. Especially considering everything that had happened. But that was exactly why another part of me wanted to stay. Now maybe finally I'd get some answers.

"I really am sorry for what I did. I know it's wrong to steal," I said, breaking the ice.

My father looked at me. I mean, really looked at me. Like he was seeing me for the first time or something. It made me nervous and I looked away.

"I didn't realize you were so unhappy," he finally said.

Hearing it out loud, I realized that I *was* "so unhappy," even though I'd never said those words or thought them, really. It felt like the words were bouncing off the doors and walls and echoing through the halls. It was as if the words themselves hurt. I could feel it in the pit of my stomach. I felt a lump rising in my throat and I swallowed hard to make it go away.

"I should be apologizing to you," he said softly.

I didn't know what to say. I looked away to hide the tears beginning to well up in my eyes. My father reached over and turned me towards him. "It hurts, doesn't it?" I nodded and reached for a napkin to wipe my face. He took my hand in his and squeezed it real hard. We sat like that for a few moments. Then my father looked down at the book in front of him. I could see now that it was some kind of photo album.

He took a deep breath and looked at me again. I could tell he was hesitating. "Okay," he finally said. "Have a look." He pushed the album over to me.

I looked at the pictures on the page. There was one shot of a woman pushing a little boy on a swing and another one of her hugging him close to her face. The little boy kind of reminded me of Mandy. He had the same curly brown hair and green eyes. The woman wore a scarf on her head like Mrs. Klein, like she was religious. I looked more closely at the little boy and noticed that he wore a *kippa*. I couldn't imagine why my father had pictures of these people.

"Who are they?" I asked

My father flipped the pages of the album back to the beginning. "Look," he said. There was a picture of a bride and groom. At first glance I couldn't tell who it was. But when I looked closer I recognized the bride as the woman in the other pictures.

"Why do you have all these photos of her?" I asked.

"Look closer at the picture," my father said. I looked again. "Now tell me who the man is."

The man had a beard and he also wore a *kippa*. He was young. Slowly I recognized the eyes, nose, and mouth. I knew them well. It felt as if my heart were going to pop right out of my chest, it was thumping so fast and hard. "That's you," I said, looking up at my father.

Chapter 20

"*I* thought I heard voices in here." It was Mom. She entered the kitchen yawning and rubbing her eyes.

I didn't know what to say to her or my father. My mind was racing a million miles a minute, trying to put the pieces together.

"Libby found me looking at these," Dad began. "She should know." My mother sat down next to my father and squeezed his hand. I liked seeing her do that.

"And Sheila. Libby, go and wake her," my father said.

"But she's mad at me. She won't listen."

"Tell her I sent you."

I went into Sheila's room and shook her. It always took forever to wake her up. She could sleep through an earthquake.

"Sheila, wake up!" I shouted. She didn't budge. "Sheila, come on..." I said again, shaking her really hard.

"Doooonnn't," she mumbled, rolling over.

"Sheila, Dad wants you."

"What are you talking about? What time is it anyway?" she said, sitting up and rubbing her eyes.

I looked at her clock. "Twelve fifteen. Come on. They're waiting for you."

"They already grounded me for four weekends in a row thanks to you. What more do you want?"

"No. It's not about that. It's about Dad." I told her about finding him in the kitchen looking at the album. I told her about the pictures I'd seen.

"What pictures? What are you talking about?"

"Just hurry up!" I said and headed back to the kitchen.

*   *   *

"Is everybody crazy?" Sheila asked, stumbling into the kitchen.

"Come sit down," my father said. I couldn't remember the last time we'd all sat together like this around our kitchen table. Dad put the album in front of Sheila and me. We began to flip slowly through the pages.

"The woman's name was Rachel. The little boy was Daniel. The man, of course, is me," he explained.

"You!" Sheila exclaimed, finally sounding awake.

"That's what I was trying to tell you," I said.

"I was much younger," my father continued.

"And you had a beard and a...what are those little caps called?" Sheila asked.

"A *kippa*?" I said.

Sheila was really interested now. She turned the pages excitedly and stopped at the one of the bride and groom. "That's you?" she said, sounding real confused. At least I wasn't the only one. "I don't get it...unless—"

"She was my wife," my father finished for her.

Sheila and I looked at each other in disbelief. I looked at my mother. She squeezed Dad's hand.

"It was a long time ago," he said.

I was so shocked I couldn't think.

"Where are they now?" Sheila wanted to know.

My father didn't answer right away. His eyes got all watery. Sheila started to bite her pinky nail and looked at the wall. I looked down at the pictures. We'd never seen Dad cry before.

My father cleared his throat. "They're not alive anymore." Sheila and I just sat there not saying anything. My father didn't go on. He seemed to be waiting to see if we wanted to hear more. We did. I did. I asked him to tell us what happened.

As we listened to my father's story unfold, I began to feel more and more as if I were in a dream. That's the only way I can describe it. Like a dream. I knew he was sitting just a few feet away from me, but his voice seemed so distant. It was very strange. I pinched myself to make sure this was really happening. I just couldn't believe what I was hearing.

*   *   *

I imagined the whole scene in my head: Their small apartment in the Jewish section of New York City. The way my father had kissed Daniel and Rachel goodbye in the morning as he left for shul. My father going to shul! My father wearing a *kippa*! My father celebrating Shabbat with his wife Rachel and son Daniel. I imagined them sitting around the dinner table, the Shabbat candles burning...burning...I felt myself sweating. I could almost feel the heat and see the blazing flames. I imagined how my father's heart must have been beating as he rounded the corner on his way home from work and heard all the fire engines. The expression he must have had on his face as he approached his building and saw it going up in flames. I felt like I had when I'd found out about Katrina. I couldn't imagine anything so horrible happening to someone so close to me.

*   *   *

I looked back at the pictures. Daniel looked a lot like Mandy. "I can't believe it," I kept saying.

"It never goes away," my father said. Tears were streaming down his cheeks. My mother kept squeezing his hand. I looked at Sheila. Tears filled her eyes.

"I'm sorry I haven't been a very good father," he continued. "Or a husband," he said, looking at my mother. "Once you've lost something you love...you're always afraid...you...." He was having trouble saying what he meant. He stopped, searching for the words. "If you don't get too close..." he continued, "...you don't have as much to lose."

What happened next is hard to describe. Something strange and funny. Maybe you really had to be there to understand it. Everyone looked around at each other. We were all sniffling and blowing our noses. Then, for some reason, it struck everybody's funny bone and we all started to laugh. My family, all together, crying and laughing from one minute to the next. I couldn't say exactly how at that moment, but I knew in my heart that things were going to be different. Mr. Goldblum was right about knowing things in your heart. And that night my heart felt so light, I thought it just might float right up through my body, out of my mouth, and into the sky.

Chapter 21

THE next morning I slept later than I ever had. It was almost lunchtime when I woke up. I jumped out of bed, hoping my dad would be around. There was still so much I wanted to talk to him about. Everything was finally beginning to make sense.

I was just pulling my shirt over my head when my mother popped her head into my room. She came over and sat down on my bed. "You still have this old thing?" she said, picking up my Raggedy Ann doll.

I told her I was saving it for when I had a daughter of my own, so that it would remind me how it felt to be young. She thought it was a wise idea. "It's so easy to forget," she admitted. I couldn't remember the last time my mother had sat on my bed with me, just talking and being together.

"Is Dad up yet?" I asked, anxious to talk more with him.

"That's what I came in to tell you. He had a

business trip. With everything that happened I forgot to tell you." Mom could see the disappointment on my face. "I'm sorry," she said, stroking my hair. "I know there are still some things you'd like to discuss with him." I nodded. I had hoped we'd be able to be together as a family that day. It just seemed liked the thing to do after last night. But I guess everything couldn't change overnight.

My mother got up to leave. "Do you think about them a lot?" I asked.

She stopped and sat back down. She knew what I meant. "Once in a while," she answered.

"Does Dad?"

"He tries very hard not to."

"So why did he keep the album?"

My mother thought for a moment. "I guess because there's a part of him that doesn't want to forget. He loved them. Like he loves us."

He loves us. Those words rang over and over in my head. My mother and I sat in silence for a few moments. There was something I wanted to know. "Does he love us as much?" I asked.

My mother looked at me. Her eyes filled with tears. She leaned over and hugged me so tight I thought she'd never let go.

Chapter 22

MY dad was due back on Sunday. On Friday I asked my mother if I could light Shabbat candles in my room. I had a feeling she wouldn't mind, now that she knew how much it meant to me. I was right. In fact, she came in and watched me light them. I used real long candles so they were still burning when I got into bed that night. I lay awake for a while, watching them burn and flicker against the dark glass. What a nice way to fall asleep. But then, just as I was dozing off, there was a quiet knock at my door. I sat up in bed to see who it was.

"Libby, are you still up?"

"Dad! What are you doing home?"

"We finished a few days early," he said, coming in. I saw him look at the candles burning in the window. By now they were very small. They probably wouldn't burn for much longer. I waited to see what he would do. He came over to my bed and sat down on the end. I propped myself up against my pillows.

"You're not going to blow them out?" I asked.

"No, I'm not."

My father picked up my Raggedy Ann doll. "I remember this," he said. "You used to take it everywhere with you."

"I know."

"How old are you now?" he asked.

"Eleven."

"It's so easy to lose track," Dad said with a deep sigh. He rose and stood in front of the candles. Now that his secret was out, I understood him better. But there was still a lot I wanted him to explain. If now wasn't the time to talk, I didn't know when it would be.

"Dad?" I began. My father looked over at me. "When you were the way you used to be, you know, like in the pictures," I paused to gather my thoughts, "you used to keep Shabbat and everything, right?" He nodded.

"Didn't you like it? I mean, how could you not?"

My father sat back down on my bed. "Of course I liked it. The food, the songs, the candles, family...I'd forgotten how much..." his voice drifted off in the middle of his sentence. I could see his mind wandering. I wished I could jump inside to see his memories.

"So why did you have to stop?" I asked quietly.

My dad looked at me. He sighed deeply. "You have to understand, Libby. When you've been through what I've been through, it shakes your very foundations. All my life I'd been raised to believe in a God who was good and fair. If you lived by His

Torah, did the right thing, and lived a good life, God would take care of you. 'No harm would befall you,' to use the words in the song we sang at the Kleins'."

I remembered the conversation my father'd had with Mr. Klein on Shabbat. Now I knew what he'd been getting at. This was just what Mr. Goldblum and I had talked about so many times. I knew what my father meant. When I thought about what had happened to both him and Mr. Goldblum, I was filled with doubts about God, too. On the other hand, I couldn't deny the feeling I had deep down in my heart about God. That He really was there. Why couldn't my father find it in his heart to go on believing in God, like Mr. Goldblum had?

"But Mr. Goldblum says that just because bad things happen to people doesn't mean that God isn't there," I said.

"Mr. Goldblum?"

I'd forgotten my father didn't know anything about Mr. Goldblum. I told him all about my old friend.

"This Mr. Goldblum may have his opinions. It's very easy for people to talk. They don't understand."

"But he does!" I jumped in. "He lost Katrina, his daughter, in Auschwitz! She was only my age. And he was in Treblinka. And his wife couldn't have any more children."

My dad was silent. He was looking at the Shabbat candles. "I didn't know you knew about Auschwitz."

"Mr. Goldblum told me."

My father shook his head. "It's amazing that he can still have such faith."

I wanted to share with my dad all that Mr. Goldblum and I had talked about. To help him understand how Mr. Goldblum was able to go on believing even after what he'd suffered. It was hard to remember everything, but I told my father as much as I could about our conversation about the Holocaust. About Yankel and the dancing men, about God being in their hearts, about saying the *Shema*, about *Olam Haba*. My father listened quietly.

"Mr. Goldblum says the good and bad all happen for the best. But sometimes we won't understand why until later...until we enter *Olam Haba*. And I think he's right. Just because we don't understand something doesn't mean God isn't there. If you believe that He is, and that He really loves us and wants what's best for us, then you have to believe that even when we suffer it's for our own good in the end. Like when I was a little girl and you wouldn't let me have candy or ice cream every time I wanted it. I thought you were so mean and such a bad father. I didn't understand. But now I know you were just doing what was best for me."

I listened to my own words. They even surprised me. I didn't know where the idea about the ice cream and candy had come from, but I liked it. I hadn't known that I really believed all this until now. But I did, I really did. And it felt good to know where I stood.

My father let out a deep sigh and stood up slowly. He stretched and walked over to my win-

dow. What could he be thinking? I held my Raggedy Ann close to me and squeezed her tight.

"Good understanding gives grace, but the way
of the faithless is rough," my dad finally said softly,
almost to himself.

"What?" I asked.

"It's from the book of Proverbs. It was the last
thing my father said to me before he died."

"What does it mean?"

I could see my dad reflected in the window.
The flames of the candles cast an orange glow on
his face.

"It can mean different things to different people.
That's the beauty of a proverb."

"Well what do you think it means?" I persisted.

"I've carried those words around with me for
ten years. I've turned them upside down and inside out," Dad said thoughtfully. "I always thought
my father was trying to warn me that if I lost faith,
I would also lose God's grace and my 'way would
be rough,' as it says. But nothing seemed farther
from the truth. It seemed like I'd already lost God's
grace. I couldn't imagine how much rougher life
could be."

My dad turned to look at me again. I could see
now that his eyes were filled with tears. He blinked
them away and cleared his throat. "But maybe my
father was trying to tell me that when a person
loses faith, it's because he lacks a proper understanding of God's ways. Like you said, Libby.
About the candy and ice cream."

Dad paused again and I smiled at him. He came

back over to me and sat down. "Perhaps what happened was God's grace," he said quietly. "All this time, I've been focusing on the loss. But what about the gain? You and Mandy and Sheila. Your mother. You wouldn't be here. Perhaps God thought it best that they should die...so you should live...for whatever reasons." He took my hand in his. "My father was a very wise man," he continued, then stopped again, as if having trouble putting his thoughts into words. He looked down at our hands. "And people make mistakes. We run away from what we don't understand. We run away from pain and anything that reminds us of it. When I came in that night and heard you saying the blessing over the candles, I hadn't heard those words in so long. It brought everything back." He looked back up at me.

I couldn't think of what to say. I felt kind of strange inside. As if all my emotions were being jumbled together and tossed around like laundry in a washing machine. I felt thanks and regret all at once. Regret because of what had happened. But thanks because...well, because of what had happened. I mean us. Me and my sisters and my mother. Like my father had said. But especially, I felt happy that Dad didn't seem to be angry at God anymore. I began to wonder what all this meant.

"So what now?" I finally asked.

My father looked at me and squinted, imitating my expression. Then he broke into a smile. "What now? Sleep, that's what now," he said, mussing my hair and tickling me back onto my pillow. He kissed my forehead and tucked my blanket in around me, just like he used to do when I was little. On his way out he turned to look at the candles one more time. It was almost midnight and they were still burning!

"What are they, magic candles?" he said.

"I used real long ones," I answered.

"I'll say...well, goodnight, Libby."

"You mean, good Shabbos," I called back.

"Good Shabbos," I heard him whisper as he closed my door.

I couldn't sleep. There was too much to think about. My father's words echoed in my head. "People make mistakes." I looked over at my window. Maybe they *were* magic candles. After all, if I'd never lit them, my father never would have gotten angry and forbidden me to go to Rebecca's. And Mom wouldn't have invited her over. And I wouldn't have gone to the art fair and seen the painting. Then I'd never have stolen the money or run away to the Kleins'. And my parents wouldn't have ended up at their Shabbat table, and my father might never have faced his past.

I got out of bed and pressed my face against my window. The moon was just a sliver and there were a million stars twinkling against the black sky. God was out there, somewhere. But where? Why didn't He make Himself visible? I looked at the reflection of the candles against the dark glass. Then again, maybe He did. Like Mr. Goldblum had said, God shows Himself in many lights. I smiled at my own reflection and shook my head. Magic candles? No. I was standing in the light of God's grace.